SUCH A
GOOD
MAN

SUCH A

GOOD

MAN

a novel

by

BRUCE K BECK

AUDACITY BOOKS

WE DARE TO TELL THE TRUTH

New York

This book is dedicated to all who fight
against intolerance.

Chapter One

Was I nervous about turning forty? Not in the least. I greeted the milestone with open arms. I had long yearned for growth and progress in my life. I read a novel once where the narrator called turning forty "a chance at maturity, but without the wrinkles." Or something like that. I agreed. I felt ready. Until that strange Wednesday afternoon.

I shouldn't have been shocked to see George Adler for the first time in nearly twenty years. We both lived in New York City, after all. More than 8.5M citizens, and yet everyone expects to have a surprise meeting with an old friend or acquaintance nearly every day. But my surprise at seeing George was visceral.

"Paul Cornell, what a treat to see you!" George said. We greeted each other warmly. I didn't want the embrace to end. As we held each other close, I drank in George's scent and wondered how I had survived the last years without it—without George filling my senses. We held each other at arm's length, smiling broadly. It was time for me to weigh in:

"George, you look fabulous!" I said. He did, of course. A few silver threads had appeared amid the glowing perfection of his dark hair, but all in the right places. Otherwise, he was unchanged. I doubted I could say the same for myself. "I can't think why we haven't run into each other in all these years, but I'm very glad to see you." I was, of course. Among other feelings.

"Paul, I've got to run to a meeting, but will you have dinner with me, maybe Friday?"

"I'd like that," I said. We exchanged numbers, and George promised to text me with the details. And then we both got on with our lives. But I felt that mine had been suddenly altered. Simple functions like breathing and walking required my attention. I got myself—focusing carefully—to my office. There was a light workload waiting on my desk, so I had time for reflection. And then I went home early.

George and I met when we were undergrads at Columbia. It was a comparative literature class. I was an English major flirting with the idea of the Episcopal priesthood, and George was similarly working toward a liberal arts degree while flirting with the rabbinate. But soon we were flirting with each other as well.

George sat across from me in that class, just to my left. It was his mouth, I think, that first caught my attention. Generous. His lips went from smiling to brooding as easily as a passing cloud could obscure the golden flecks in his eyes. I wanted to own George's mouth. I wanted to have it for my personal use only. I wanted to be free to kiss him at will.

I settled for a few dates and then a few tosses in his bed or mine. We had—a flirtation? No, it was more than that. I took his dick in my mouth, after all. My first? My first reasonably adult dick, anyway. I loved having it there. So, did we have an affair, George and I? I suppose it was less than that.

I've often wondered if it was just a post-adolescent fantasy. But no, that's not the truth either. *My* truth is that I would have committed myself to George, body and soul, if he had asked me to. To hell with God! I'd have happily worshiped *George* for the rest of my life. There! I've said it.

It was a sweet time. But one day, George's mother phoned to tell him his father was dying of some sort of awful illness and that he had to come home. And that was that. I tried not to dwell on it. My Buffalo, NY, childhood gave me ample training in stuffing feelings. I stuffed. I finished my BA and went off to law school—rather than the seminary. And still I stuffed. And I never heard from George. He could have written to me. I certainly wrote to him. We were still writing letters in those days. Just barely.

All this history flashed before my eyes as I headed home that Wednesday afternoon. It was Jason's evening to make dinner, but I was home so early that I went to the fridge and found the groceries he had laid in. As I started in on our meal, I revisited the past. I felt miserable, as if the last two decades had been wasted. Squandered. As if my life had no foundation, really. As if my house of cards had collapsed and left me pinned under the rubble. "Jesus fucking Christ!" I said to myself. "Why George? Why now?"

After Jason arrived home and kissed me, he took a good look and said, "What's wrong, Pauly? You look as if you'd seen a ghost."

"I did, actually," I said. "It's nothing. I started dinner. Why don't you change and come have a drink with me? I missed you today." It was the truth.

"I miss *you* whenever we're apart, Pauly," he said. "I'll be right out." Jason headed for the bedroom to slip out of his exercise wear and into shorts and a T. He looked beautiful whatever he was wearing. And most beautiful when he was wearing nothing at all. It was the perfection of his body that first attracted me. No surprise there. I invited Jason into my bed because he was gloriously hunky, but I asked him to stay because of his sweet nature.

Jason was a personal trainer—*my* personal trainer. I felt mildly silly about having an affair with my trainer, but I got over it. Jason was smart and kind and eager to please—eager to be my partner. He had even let me drag him to the opera a few times. We had been dating for maybe two months or so when I asked him to move in with me. "Paul, are you sure?" he asked. "That's pretty serious. I've wanted it for a while now, but I'm not so certain about you." This was wisdom coming from a man ten years my junior.

"Quite sure," I said. "I want you here. I want you to be mine, if you'll have me." Jason assured me I was exactly what he wanted in his life, and we did the deed. That was two years ago. I never regretted our decision to merge. And yet I wondered how much I really had to offer Jason. He freely gave me his beautiful body and his beautiful soul, and I gave him—what? And yet Jason told me he was happy, and that made me happy. And that's where my life was that strange Wednesday.

"Pauly, come to bed," Jason said to me after we had had dinner and cleaned up. "You look tired. We can go to sleep right away if you want." When we had turned out the lights and settled into bed, he said, "Let me hold you." Jason was a marvel of a man. Everything about him was pure strength, except for the part that was pure devotion. And *that* was pure strength, too. Jason always knew, instinctively, what I needed from him. He could pet me and coddle me, he could throw me down onto the bed and fuck the shit out of me, or he could welcome me into his arms and into his body with perfect submission.

I wanted Jason. Intensely. That Wednesday night. He responded. He wrapped his strong legs around my waist and encouraged me to inhabit him. When I had taken possession, he clung to me and said, "I love you, Paul." I started to cry, but only just a little. I chalked it up to passion. I made love to Jason as simply and as purely as perhaps I ever had. I kissed him as deeply as I ever had, surely. And when I offered up the sacramental fluid, he received it reverently.

When we had recovered a little and headed to the bathroom to clean up, Jason said, "Jesus, Pauly! You were magnificent."

"Thanks, Jason, but I'm not sure how I did that," I said. "So don't expect a repeat performance." Jason snapped my butt with his towel, so of course I had to chase him down and demand a kiss by way of apology. We hadn't engaged in locker-room antics maybe ever. It felt light. It was the two of us. Together. I sensed it was the closest we had been in the last year, maybe. I liked it. I think Jason liked it even more.

Bruce K Beck

When we had returned to the bedroom and settled in again, I spooned Jason and held him as close
to me as I could. "Sweet Jesus!" I said to myself.
"Look at this perfect man in my arms. I know I don't
deserve him, but please, can I keep him?" I'm not
very good at prayer. I'd be in a different line of work
if I were. I gave up on trying to pray and slept instead.

Chapter Two

In the morning, Jason had an early client. He was up and out by 6:30. I went back to bed and napped for a half hour, and then I started my day with coffee and *THE NEW YORK TIMES*. I was in no hurry. I phoned Clyde—my best friend Clyde Hutchings. I had to tell him about seeing George.

"So, what are you going to do about this?" Clyde asked.

"Besides having dinner with George tomorrow night?"

"Besides having dinner with George tomorrow night."

"I don't know yet, Clyde," I said. "I don't know what he wants from me. He probably intends to tell me all about his career and his wife and his children. The eldest is probably about to apply to Harvard. Who knows?"

"You've been soft on George for a lot of years, Paul. I knew it when we were dating. In fact, I often felt there was a third man in our bed—and not in a good way. I don't see that anything has changed much through the years. Please be careful. I'd hate to see you fuck it up with Jason," Clyde said. "Don't imagine that men of his quality are waiting around every corner—especially for old men like us."

"Thank you, dear," I said. "I can always count on you for a cheery message."

"You can always count on me to tell you the truth, Pauly. As you very well know."

"And that's part of why I love you so much. Thanks, Clyde," I said, "I'll call you Saturday." I had been honest with Clyde. I had no idea where this George business was going. But then, nothing had happened more than a chance meeting. So there was really nothing to think about. More or less.

Thinking of Clyde always brought a smile to my lips. He knew me better than anyone. Before or since. We were in our early twenties when we met one night at a club. Clyde was so fresh and vital. His openness melted my Buffalo reserve. I was smitten. We dated for a while. We tried all those acrobatic things that twentysomethings need to try. The sex was great. We even lived together for a year. But it became apparent to both of us that sex was not to be the basis of our relationship. We found a different sort of love. And it has never wavered.

I phoned my secretary and asked him to transfer my calls to my cell phone. "I'll be working from home today," I said. That was a fairly odd concept at the time, but he agreed. That left me to savor the morning quiet. I've always marveled at how peaceful the city can seem in a high-rise apartment with double-glazed windows. I let the quiet and the morning sunlight wash over me. I was in no hurry to alter the pace.

I did take some business calls that day, but I didn't need to meet with anyone from the Diocese. And I certainly didn't have to be in court. I'll back up. I told you I went to law school. I did well, actually. And passed the bar on the first try. I got some odd jobs clerking here and there. It was a living, and it gave me freedom to travel a bit—on a tight budget—and to consider what I really wanted to do when I grew up. If I grew up.

And then five years ago I was offered a position as an attorney for the Episcopal Diocese of New York. I'd have accepted the job even if the diocesan offices had not been close to the Cathedral Church of St. John the Divine—one of the most glorious manifestations of faith in the world. I wasn't so certain of my faith, but I was willing to take the job and to see if maybe some of the glory of that structure and its mission might rub off on me. The jury is still out.

That quiet Thursday, I headed out to go food shopping in the early afternoon. A little Zabar's, a little Citarella, a little Trader Joe's. I wanted to make something special for Jason's dinner. Clyde's admonition was not wasted on me. I got it. I wondered how warm and open I had been in the last months. And I wanted to be a better partner. That was it, really.

When Jason got home, I said, "Go change for dinner, you great sweaty brute. But don't remove a drop of sweat. Let me see." I lifted Jason's arms, pulled up his shirt, and dove for his right armpit. "Delicious," I said. "Yes, I want it all." Jason kissed me and headed to the bedroom. I poured an Italian red and put the mussels on to steam. I had already toasted big chunks of good bread, rubbed them with a garlic clove, and anointed them with too much good green olive oil. I had also made a salad with chickpeas and very sweet grape tomatoes in rainbow colors. And It wasn't even June.

When Jason returned and joined me at the kitchen counter, I kissed him in earnest, and then I sat him down and served up dinner. "Pauly, this is delicious," he said. "Can we have this every night?"

"Sure, if you want to end up looking like an Italian grandmother."

"I could do worse," he said.

"Much worse. But I want you exactly as you are. Let's vary the diet." I wanted to mention my plan to vary *my* diet the following evening, but I wasn't ready to tell Jason I had a dinner date. I knew, of course, that the longer I put it off, the harder it would be to mention, casually, that I would not be home for dinner on Friday. And yet I waited.

"Clyde sends love," I said over coffee.

"I always liked Clyde best of all your friends," Jason said.

"That's easy. I've often felt you should have fallen in love with Clyde instead of me," I said. "He's such a good man."

Jason grabbed me and said, "Pauly, how can you say that? You know how I feel about you. You know you're everything I've ever wanted. Take it back."

"I'm sorry, Jase," I said. "That was a stupid remark. And it isn't even true—I mean the part about my thinking you should have fallen in love with Clyde instead of me. I'd have been devastated if you had. The part about Clyde being the better man is gospel, however."

"I don't do so well with scripture, Pauly," Jason said, "not since my grandfather used to beat me while quoting it."

I lunged for Jason and held him as tightly as I dared. "I think I need to find a new vocabulary, perfect man. But not tonight. We don't really need words tonight," I said. "Will you let me take charge?" Jason smiled. I led him to the bedroom. I slipped off his clothes, and mine, and invited Jason to lie in the middle of our bed. His beauty had often made me weep in the last two years. Never more than that Thursday night.

I lay on top of Jason, with my full weight, and kissed him deeply, to start. And then I began to explore—re-explore—that muscled terrain I knew so well. I even knew how Jason achieved the delicate perfection of it. But understanding the process does nothing to diminish the splendor of the result. Just because I know how Crater Lake was formed doesn't mean that I'm less awed by it. Maybe even more so?

I tried to honor Jason's body—with my hands, with my mouth, with whatever other body parts of mine I could use to administer gentle attention. I caressed his arms and his hands. I took my time with both armpits. They had been among my favorite parts of his body since our first date. I might have stalled there, except I knew I had begun to tickle him, and that was not my intention.

Nipples are marvels of engineering, of course. Men's nipples are especially exciting to me because they seem to exist solely for pleasure. And Jason's pleasure was my only focus that Thursday night. I worked my way down his sculpted torso. Ah, Jason's dick! In size, shape, and function, it was just as perfect as the rest of him. Had I honored it properly—in the last few months? Had I honored Jason properly? Probably not. I hoped to correct the oversight.

I've always loved balls. Jason's weren't huge, but who needs huge balls? Carrying them around is too much work, I'm told. I wouldn't know. Jason's were perfect, like the rest of him. They were always present. Available for worship or play. I once asked

Jason—when we were dating—to let me sleep with my face in his crotch. We're not talking 69 here. Nothing so obvious as that. I simply wanted to spend the night in that heady zone between Jason's flawless legs.

He was good natured about it. He was always good natured, of course. Was that the night that made me decide to ask Jason to move in? Maybe. But I did ask, and he accepted me. And as a result, I had access to my favorite real estate whenever I wanted to visit it. And I most certainly wanted a lengthy visit that Thursday night. I could tell when Jason was getting close, of course. I maintained the rhythm that had advanced him to that point. He quivered with pleasure. I felt pride in my ability to effect such an event.

Just before Jason erupted, he took my face in his hands and shouted, "I love you, Pauly!" And then he delivered my favorite dessert. I savored each drop. I stayed with Jason's dick until I was certain I had brought him all possible pleasure. And then I surrendered my favorite toy and lay beside Jason. He put his arm around me. We were silent for a while.

"Thank you, Pauly." Jason broke the silence.

"Thank *you*, Jase," I said. "You always know what I need."

"I wish I did," he said. "I wish I understood you a little better, Pauly. Or a lot better, maybe. Sometimes you're light and easy. Loving. Like tonight. And last night, too. But other times you're like a stranger in your own home. I prefer tonight's version of you, but I accept the other one as well. It's probably my fault."

I grabbed Jason with both hands and said, "Nothing is your fault, Jase. Ever. You're perfect. I've always known that. But I've never been much good at telling you how precious you are to me. I'm working on it."

"Our bed is a perfect place for that kind of work. I have another early morning, Pauly. Do you want to brush teeth and call it a night?" And that's what we did. I felt blessed to have Jason in my arms for yet another night of peaceful slumber. I also felt vaguely like an impostor. And I felt like a coward for not telling Jason about my dinner date with George. Telling him would have to wait. Maybe I could text him at noon to tell him about a last-minute business meeting. That seemed plausible. I'd think of something, surely. Meanwhile, I had everything I needed in my arms. Sleep claimed me.

<u>*Chapter Three*</u>

I decided to go with the noontime text about a surprise dinner meeting. Jason said he'd grab a bite after work with his colleagues, Marvin and Lisa. He was good-natured about it, of course. I felt like a rat. I also felt compelled to see George again. I couldn't think of a way to balance the two desires— wanting to be good and kind to Jason and needing to dredge up my past.

George and I met at 7:00 at a very handsome modern Italian restaurant—at 65th & Madison, I think it was. Spiffy, welcoming, comfortable chairs, an inviting garden in the back. George had reserved a table overlooking the garden but still within the air- conditioned comfort of the dining room. Perfect. I was glad to be in a suit and tie. It felt like light ar- mor—a way to distance the heart and keep it safe. "I wondered if I'd see you again, Paul," George said. "I've wanted to."

I smiled. I couldn't voice it, but I said to myself, "And yet you never wrote, George. You never reached out."

"You really do look terrific, Paul. I could have picked you out of a crowd. Easily. But I don't really know what you've been up to. Is it nineteen years now?" Instead of reminding George of how easy it would have been for him to remain in my life—even long distance—I gave him the capsule version: law school, odd jobs, travel, and then settling down at the Diocese. Jason, of course. That was about it.

"I know nothing about *your* life, George," I said.

"Yes, well, after Dad's death I had to reconsider everything. I had no idea who I was. The only certainty in my life was that I had fallen wildly in love with you, Paul." I winced, I'm sure. "It didn't seem viable. They didn't have gay rabbis in those days. I didn't really think of myself as gay, to be honest. Probably still don't. But I knew I couldn't go back to Columbia—back to the life we shared. So I transferred credits and did an MBA at MIT. That's where I met Sarah. You'd like her, Paul. She's beautiful, smart, accomplished, a wonderful mother. She'd *love* you. You're much more her type than I am.

"I took a job in the business office at Temple Emanu-El. We moved to New York—to Rye, actually. There was a lot that was good in our marriage, including two beautiful children. But it wasn't enough. And five years ago we decided to pack it in. Sarah is still parenting, of course, and she seems to thrive on the civic work she does in Westchester. I show up at the Temple and do my job, and then I go home, alone. I see the kids on alternate weekends. I don't know another way to do it. I wondered if maybe you could teach me how to love again, the way you taught me twenty years ago."

Fuck! I thought. By then we had gotten through two lovely courses and were enjoying a delicious *tiramisu* that was spiked with raspberry liqueur. I pushed it aside. "Could I have another glass of wine?" I asked.

"Of course," George said. "I'm going to order a brandy. Will you have one?"

"Sure," I said. I sat. I drank. I fidgeted.

"The ball is in your court, Paul," George said. I looked at the handsome man across the table from me, and I realized that he was hardly a relic from my past. George was perfectly alive and devastatingly attractive. His mouth called to me as loudly as it had called to me in literature class. I think I shivered, slightly, as I tried to process the sensations. George put his hand on the table, as if inviting me to hold it. I couldn't do it.

"What did you think, George?" I asked. "What did you think was happening, back at Columbia? I know exactly how much I adored you, and yet, I was never certain of your feelings."

"I thought you were the friend I'd never had, Paul. The *brother* I never had and always wanted. I also thought you were the most beautiful creature I'd ever laid eyes on. That's what I thought. Your hair in the sunlight, and your eyes when you looked at me. I wanted to possess you, Paul, and I wanted to *be* you, maybe all at the same time. That's what I thought."

I was silent for rather a long while. Coffee arrived. Another brandy. We sat. And finally I asked, "Why, George? Why the silence all these years?"

"That's a fair question," George said. "I thought I had to make a clean break with my past, when I went back home. And then I reinvented myself. And then I thought I had nothing to offer you. Even in the years since my divorce. I knew you were at the Diocese, Paul. I knew I could reach you. I couldn't do it. I wouldn't have dared. I felt so much shame about leaving you in silence. But when we met on Wednesday, it felt like a sign from the Universe. Like permission to see you again."

"Thanks for that, George," I said after I finished my second brandy. "I really should be getting home. Jason is waiting for me. You should meet him, George. Jason is ... perfect, actually. Thanks for dinner." We rose to leave. I felt a brain fog out of proportion to the (excessive) number of drinks I had consumed. It was George, of course. We headed to the street.

"I live just a block from here, Paul. Will you come up for a few minutes?" George asked.

"No, thank you. Not tonight," I said. Not tonight? What was I thinking? *No* is a complete sentence.

"Well then, next time, maybe," George said. "I hope there'll be a next time. I want to see you again, Paul. I meant what I said about wanting to put things right."

"I have a life, George," I said. "Please don't ask me to upend it."

"I don't want anything but your happiness, Paul. That's all I ever wanted. But I couldn't figure out how to give you that in the past. I think I could do it, now. Will you trust me?"

"That sounds a little crazy, even to me," I said.

"Well then, will you kiss me?" he asked. I did, of course. "Yes, that's it, Paul. That's what I've been missing all these years. Promise me you'll think about it. Promise me you'll give me a chance to get it right this time."

"I promise," I said, and then I got into the first cab I could find to speed me back to the West Side.

When I got home, Jason was preparing for bed. I kissed him, and he said, "I don't like it when you drink too much. It isn't good for you. And it makes me sad. Go, brush your teeth, Pauly, and come to bed." That sobered me up a little. I did as I was told.

When I slipped between the sheets and spooned the perfect man lying beside me, he said, "I miss you when you're away, Pauly. Especially when you're away while you're lying next to me."

I started to weep. I said, "Please don't give up on me, Jase."

"Hush, baby," he said. "Get some sleep." Jason snuggled in tightly against my body. I soon slipped into unconsciousness.

Chapter Four

The weekend was chilly. In my apartment, I mean. Outdoors, summer continued unabated. I tried to pretend that my Saturday morning hangover was nothing. Jason knew better. He was kind, of course, and he made me one of those tomato juice shots with tabasco and a raw egg in it. It helped.

Clyde phoned and suggested an outing. He was spending the day with our friend, Lily, and he wondered if we might like to join them. I thought that an excellent idea. So did Jason. We agreed to meet at the Boathouse in Central Park at noon.

When we met up, Lily grabbed Jason's hand and said. "Come and help me feed the ducks. Just don't let anyone see us. It's probably illegal." Lily adored Jason. It was love at first sight for the two of them. I think she liked Jason far better than she liked Clyde and me—and we were the two who shared more than a decade of history with her. We met here when she first moved to New York—a difficult time when people have to develop a new support network. Clyde and I were delighted to provide that.

"Let the youngsters scamper along," Clyde said. "I want some news."

"Yes, well, I met George for dinner last night." Clyde looked patient. "Italian. It was delicious."

Clyde looked less patient. "We talked." Clyde brightened. "About the past, at Columbia."

"You'd better come clean, young man," Clyde said. "This conversation is getting us nowhere."

"Quite right," I said. "Clyde, I was so shocked. George told me had always loved me and that he disappeared because he didn't think he could give me what I deserve. Now he thinks he can. And he wants to try. He wants to atone, really."

"Sweet Jesus, Pauly," Clyde said. "You certainly can pick 'em. What are you going to do?"

"Nothing, of course," I said. "I love my life. I wouldn't do anything to put it at risk."

"Is it that easy, Paul?" Clyde asked. "Can you just walk away from the man who has held your heart for twenty years? At this point I can't think of anything short of an exorcism that would free you of George. I hope I'm wrong."

"I'm *sure* you're wrong, Clyde," I said. "It was good to gain some clarity. It was comforting, I suppose, to learn that I hadn't *imagined* the past, that George loved me as much as I loved him. And now, there's an end to it, and I can move on."

"I hope you're right, dear," Clyde said. "And speaking of moving on, let's collect the kiddies and go in for some brunch."

"Good thinking," I said. Lily and Jason were laughing and playing on the edge of the lake. Jason was radiant in the summer sunlight. He was such a little boy in so many ways, and yet such a wise old man in others. I knew how lucky I was to have his love. I understood. I only hoped that what I told Clyde about moving on was the truth. I hoped I could get a grip on my heart and make it behave.

We had a pleasant afternoon. The brunch was adequate, and the view was better. It was always fun to be with Lily. Interesting woman. She had a trust fund—so she knew she'd never miss a meal—plus she started a company providing services for busy New Yorkers. Lily arranged all sorts of things for her clients, including food, flowers, fashions, theater tickets, house cleaning, wine deliveries, and dog walking. For a fee, of course. Jason got some of his best house-call clients through Lily. She was successful. She deserved it.

After brunch, we decided on a good long walk in the park. At one point, Jason and Clyde walked a little ahead of Lily and me. She took my arm and smiled sweetly. "You look like shit, Pauly," she said through her smile. "Jason says it's a hangover. What do you say?" Lily was never one to mince words.

"Have you ever known Jason to be wrong?"

"Never," Lily said.

"Well, there you have it." I knew that wasn't enough. I knew my old friend deserved an explanation. But I didn't have one handy. Opening up to Clyde was about as much soul-searching as I was prepared to pursue in one day.

"Look, Pauly," she said. "You know I love you. And I want everything that's best for you. But if you make Jason unhappy, I swear I'll come for you, and I'll cut off your balls. I know where you keep them. I have my methods."

I stopped there, in the middle of the trail, and looked Lily straight in the eye. I said, "Lily, Jason's happiness is the most important thing in my life. I couldn't do anything to jeopardize that."

"See that you don't. I'll pray for you, Father."

"Bless you, my child," I said. "I'll take all the prayer I can get." I looked ahead and asked Lily, "Where do you think the boys got to? Maybe they've disappeared into the Ramble."

"Old habits die hard," Lily said. "I'll bet we can catch up to them." And that's what we did. The four of us wandered for a while and then left the park right in front of Natural History. There was a temporary show about Pompeii that we all wanted to see. It was remarkable. And then it was time to head home.

Clyde and Lily were planning a pajama party at Clyde's. They invited us to join them. He had an extra bedroom, after all. It might have been fun, but I wasn't so keen on it. I was looking forward to some alone time with Jason. He sensed my feelings and echoed them. We said good-bye to our friends and headed home.

We had some food in the fridge we could cobble together to make a little supper. We talked about movies and TV. We made some choices. Nothing too heavy. We settled in for a quiet evening at home. I asked Jason to cuddle with me on the sofa. He agreed, of course, but as soon as he settled into my embrace he said, "What's wrong, Paul? Why are you so tense?"

"I wish I could explain it to you, Jase."

"I'm here, Pauly. You can tell me anything," he said. I ran it through my head: twenty years ago— the love of my life—disappeared until this week—resurfaced and wants me back. I didn't quite believe the story myself. How could I expect Jason to buy it? I tried. God knows I tried to be honest with Jason. But I couldn't do it.

Instead, I kissed him. It was a kiss with desperation in it. I knew that. Jason accepted me, just as he always had. And then I said, "I can't do it, Jason. Will you give me some time?"

"I don't know what that means, Paul," Jason said. "I thought we were always honest with each other. I thought honesty was the basis of our relationship. You're making me wonder what we've been doing the last two years. You're making me wonder if I know you at all." I reached for Jason. He didn't pull away, exactly, but he also didn't welcome my embrace.

Jason said, "Look, Paul, I don't know what's going on here, and I'm not willing to continue with this … non-conversation. I'm going to bed. Maybe you'll have something to tell me tomorrow that makes sense. I hope so."

Jason loved me. I knew he did. I never questioned it. But which me did he love? Was it the warm and generous me? Was it the playful me? Or was it the dark and brooding me? That last self I had tried to hide from him. From myself, really. With imperfect success. And what about the me who had never been able to say, "I love you," to him. Though clearly I did. What about *that* me?

One of us—or was it an amalgam?—followed Jason to bed. He let me hold him. I couldn't have stood it if he had pushed me away. I wouldn't have survived the night without Jason's presence, beside me. I pressed my face between his shoulder blades and tried to find some equilibrium in Jason's strength. I wouldn't call it sleeping, exactly—what I did that night. But morning came anyway, as it always does.

I had never spent a day with Jason barely speaking to me. Sunday was torture, and yet I still couldn't find the words that would break the spell. We had a little breakfast, we read the Sunday *NEW YORK TIMES*, we watched some old movies, we read books for a while, we relaxed—or rather, Jason relaxed. Sunday stuff.

Early in the evening I suggested we order in some takeout. I had no appetite, but that was hardly Jason's fault. He agreed to Persian, since the best Persian restaurant in the city had a branch nearby. Lamb, deep herbal flavors, saffron rice—it was all good. I ordered too much food, even though I wasn't certain who would eat it. I wanted to do something generous for Jason. I probably hoped to make peace.

Jason set the table. We had dinner mostly in silence. I didn't feel ready to have the only conversation that could clear the air—clear away the cobwebs, really. Instead I tried to be present and attentive. I needn't have bothered, of course. I made strong black tea, and we put away the—copious—leftovers. Jason and I had never shared such a bitter meal. It was all new territory.

At bedtime, Jason said, "I don't know what's going on, Paul, but I don't like it. Lily invited me to stay with her. I'm going to head out in the morning, and I'll be with her until you can tell me what I'm missing, here. I don't like being left in the dark. I'd rather be where people tell the truth. I'm not angry with you, exactly, Paul, and nothing could make me love you less, but I can't live this way. Call me. When you're ready."

It was like a kick in the gut, of course. I managed to get to bed and even to do a little sleeping, I think. And in the morning, Jason was gone before I headed to work.

Chapter Five

I phoned Clyde as soon as I got to work. "I know," he said. "Look, Paul, I can't talk now. Will you have lunch with me?" I agreed, of course. I had a miserable morning trying to review some nuisance suits against the Diocese and figure out the best way to handle them. My secretary brought me some research materials and a cup of coffee. Nice guy. Cute, too. Beautiful brown skin. Great ass.

"Is there anything else you need, Mr. Cornell?" he asked. I hated the formality, but it was part of the office culture.

"No, thank you, Jeremy," I said. "I'll be going out for lunch at noon, so please forward my calls to my cell phone until I get back."

"Sure thing, Mr. Cornell," he said. "If there's anything else you need, just ask." Jeremy smiled sweetly. Was he flirting with me? Probably. Some twentysomethings find older men attractive. Most any gay man would find Jeremy very attractive indeed. If I had been the sort of married man who has affairs, I'd have hit on Jeremy his first week on the job. But I wasn't, so I didn't.

I smiled and said, "Can't think of a thing, but thanks for the offer." Jeremy knew I was playing the game, of course. It was light. It was fun. It was harmless. And it made a welcome change from the storm going on in my heart. I slogged through the rest of the work morning. And then I put on my jacket and headed out to meet Clyde.

"How strongly did Lily trash me?" I asked over Cobb Salad and a glass of pinot grigio.

"Very," Clyde said. "But then you expected that."

"Did you tell her about George?"

"No, dear," Clyde said. "It's not my secret to tell. I think we both know who has to man up and deal with the secrets." Clearly we both *did* know whose responsibility that was. But I wasn't yet ready to accept it—or maybe to *act* on it.

"Jason said he doesn't hate me, and I'm hoping you don't either. And that you won't hate me even when I tell you I have to see George again."

"Look, Pauly, it doesn't matter what I think. You'll do exactly what you need to do, of course. It has nothing to do with me. But you want my blessing. I can't give it. I don't think you're considering the big picture. But I respect your right to make your own choices. So do what you have to do. Please be careful. And know that my love is always with you."

"Fuck!" I exclaimed, *sotto voce.* "I know I don't deserve your friendship, Clyde, but I don't know how I'd survive without it."

"Well, don't try," he said. "Just come back to us as soon as you can."

I headed to the office and floated through the afternoon drudgery. About 3:00, I texted George and asked, "Will you see me? Maybe dinner tomorrow night?" He got right back to me: "Of course, but tonight is even better." I told him I had had a big lunch and wouldn't have much appetite. "Me, too. So just come to my apartment and we'll figure something out."

I wondered if we really could figure something out, after all those years. George texted me his address. I told him I could be there by 6:00. Done.

📖

George had the second floor of an old brownstone building in the East 60s. When I rang his bell and he buzzed me in, visions of Jason danced in my head. Jason was sweeter than sugarplums any day, but I found the dance disturbing. "What the fuck are you doing?" I asked myself. And I had no reply. I walked up, and George let me in. He kissed me, of course. I loved George's kiss. I knew I would. No surprise there.

"I'm so glad you're here, Paul. Please sit, and I'll bring us a glass of wine." I liked George's apartment very much. His furniture looked comfortable and rather traditional, but stark white walls gave a very modern feel to the rooms, as well as showing off his artwork to advantage, of course. He returned with not just glasses but a bottle of wine in one of those clay coolers. An Oregon pinot gris. Luscious.

"I've imagined you here so many times, Paul," George said. "But actually having you here is even better than the fantasy."

"You have me a little off-balance, George. I'm not certain why I came. I don't think sharing a delicious wine is reason enough—as temping as it is. What's going on?"

"I want you back, Paul," George said. "It's all I've wanted for years now. Sarah knew. We didn't keep many secrets from each other. I told her about you before we were married. She was gracious. If I had been able to forget you, I think I'd still be married to Sarah. But I couldn't forget. I think that's why she divorced me, really."

"You certainly know how to cheer a guy up," I said.

"Oh, Paul, you know I'm not trying to assign blame. I'm just trying to be as honest as I can be. I don't feel I have time for bullshit anymore. Will you come to bed?"

"Yes," said my lips, while my heart said, "No, no, no." George offered me his hand, for the second time that week. I took it. He led me to his bedroom. I'm sure I knew that was where our meeting would end up. But it was still a shock to me that I could go to bed with anyone other than Jason. But Jason had left me, after all.... George kissed me—in earnest. Nothing polite. It was all about passion. I responded in kind.

We undressed quickly and got right to the business of lovemaking, just as we had done when we were twenty. Paul's body was exactly as I remembered it, only a bit more—manly? He embraced me with the same warmth. His kisses were much better than the adolescent ones we had shared back then. Everything about being in George's bed was better than any memories. We were making new ones. I knew it. And I knew that my life would never be quite the same.

George was gentle and respectful, while at the same time he was passionate and persuasive. We explored and enjoyed each other for a good long while. I took an interest in his nipples, and his dick, of course. He took an interest in my armpits. I wasn't used to that kind of attention. Eventually, George said, "Paul, there's something I've wanted to do for twenty years. We never tried it back then. Will you let me inside?"

I figured I might as well be hanged for a sheep as a lamb. I wasn't about to deny George anything. At that point, I'd have gotten on all fours and done a poodle dance, if he had asked me to. But what he asked was for me to let him top me. I submitted as graciously as I could. George got into position to enter me. There would be no hesitation. George moved my legs, gently, for maximum access. When he presented his dick, he paused to see if there was welcome in my eyes. And then he was in.

We both exclaimed. The sensation was like nothing I'd ever experienced. I'd had dick up my ass before, of course. But it was never like that. I was humbled by it. I think George was too. He shed tears that landed on my belly. Mine mostly ended up on the pillow. George inhabited me, as if he had always belonged there. As if I had always belonged to him. It wasn't far from the truth.

When George came, so did I. How could I not? Eventually the room stopped spinning and we were merely two youngish men in a very comfortable bed. "Well worth the wait," George said.

"Nineteen years is a long time to wait. What made you think I hadn't forgotten you?"

"Paul, no one could forget what we shared. Not either of *us*, anyway. I've known for years that it was only a matter of time before we found each other again. And now that we have, I'm starting to feel a little hope for the future." Hope was most certainly *not* what I was feeling. Other concepts came to mind, like anguish, failure, weakness, betrayal.

I said, "George, that was lovely, and I don't really regret a moment of it. Except that I feel so guilty."

"Hush, Paul," he said. That's *my* heritage, not yours. Let's just enjoy what we have, while we have it."

"Am I a little bit Jewish now?" I asked.

"Only if you want to be. We're not much on converts, you know." We held each other for a long while. Sometimes I needed George's kiss, and sometimes he demanded mine. We lay quietly until the summer sun had disappeared entirely. "I suppose we should think about a little supper," he said. George threw me a robe, and we adjourned to the kitchen, which was nicely appointed. "I have some eggs. Not much else. I don't eat in often."

"Then I'll scramble eggs and see if I can make them look like an omelet."

"Perfect," he said. We got to the business of supper, and within minutes we were sitting at George's dining table with my eggs and his pinot gris. It felt like a feast. We enjoyed it mostly in silence, to begin. When we were nearly finished with supper, I began to feel sad about ending my visit. I had no intention of sleeping over, but I hated to leave.

"I do know a little theology, George," I said over coffee.

"Of course you do."

"I can't see much difference in us, except that Jews stopped going to war and killing people centuries ago (never mind Israel), while Christians put on the mantle and have refused to surrender it to this day. Though Islam gives us a run for our money."

"Eloquent, my friend," George said. "May I quote you?"

"As long as you spell my name right. Two l's, you know. Better still, don't quote me. If it got back to the Diocese, it might not be well received."

"Your secret is safe with me. Your *life* is safe with me, actually. If you'll let me. Will you stay over, Paul? I'd like that very much."

"No, George. I have a lot to process tonight. And I still have to show up for work in the morning and make sense—as much as possible."

"Will you invite me to your apartment some time?"

"No, George. I bought our bed when Jason moved in, and there's never been another man in it. I wouldn't. I couldn't."

"I admire men who know their own mind. I think I've always been rather wishy-washy in mine. I put up a brave front for my wife and my children, but at heart I've always been a scared little boy. You're the only one who ever made me feel like a man, Paul."

"Fuck!" I said. "That's a lot of responsibility. Please don't say things like that to me, George."

"What should I say?" he asked.

"Tell me you like my omelet; tell me you like my ass; tell me you remember the color of my eyes and want to see them again in the sunlight. Tell me you love me. That's allowed."

"All of the above," George said. "You're much better at these things than I am. I thought lawyers were supposed to be dry and humorless."

"Not this one," I said, "I hope."

"You're the juiciest man I know, Paul. Please give me a chance." Reluctantly, I put my work clothes back on and said good night to George. It was ... difficult. But necessary. A last kiss, and I was out his door and into the street. It was a particularly sultry evening, as only August in New York can be. I'd have to get home before I could find something bracing. Maybe I'd bury my face in a sink full of ice

and vodka, the way Joan Crawford did. I also wondered how many people alive today remember Joan
Crawford. And then I stopped trying to make sense
of anything and went to bed.

Chapter Six

My sister, Maryanne, texted me in the morn-ing to tell me she would be coming to New York in a few days. There was an annual conference at the Hilton that she always attended. I should have realized I'd be seeing her soon. But I was too self-involved to remember anything that far removed from my personal drama.

I texted her back: "Lovely! You'll stay with me."

She replied, "No, Pauly. They have a room for me at the Hilton. All arranged."

I replied, "Well then un-arrange it. You're staying here."

"When did you become so decisive?"

"I take big brothering very seriously, so I always know what's best for you."

"All right, I'll change my accommodation plans, despite your macho posturing. I love you, Paul."

"Ditto! See you Friday." I texted Clyde immediately. I knew he'd want to see Maryanne. And I knew they'd work out the particulars between them.

Memories of Buffalo were never very welcome, though I adored Maryanne. She was the one bright spot in an otherwise dark childhood. I always felt I was the wrong-shaped peg, whatever the hole. Especially these days, when there are gay kids who demand acceptance—and get it. It's temperament, of course, and role models. We didn't have those. I spent much of my childhood gritting my teeth and praying for escape.

It wasn't until I got to Columbia that I started to breathe properly. It wasn't that there were faggots everywhere and I could feel proud to walk among them. I don't think any campus experience is like that, then or now. But I was granted a measure of respect for who I was. And I knew I could keep that respect as long as I earned it. I worked hard. I thrived. Even the year I fell in love with George I still did the work.

Maryanne and I both used to tell people we were distant cousins of Katherine Cornell. That meant something in Buffalo. But through the years we both realized there were not all that many people who knew who she was. So that little bit of family pride began to melt away. Good riddance to pride, I suppose.

Cornell never forgot her Buffalo childhood and always toured her plays there. She thought of herself as a true daughter of Buffalo. I couldn't find any such allegiance in *my* heart, surely. I was delighted to be living in New York City. One of the plays Cornell brought to Buffalo was her signature triumph, the role of Elizabeth in *THE BARRETTS OF WIMPOLE STREET*. It brought her a measure of immortality, but even immortals can be forgotten.

I muddled through the work week as I usually did. George waited for me to reach out. He had promised—more or less—not to stalk me. He kept his word. I texted him on Wednesday to tell him about Maryanne's visit and that I would be pretty much unavailable for the next week. He suggested dinner—something simple, on Thursday night. I accepted. I was pleased at the prospect of seeing him again, of course, but equally disturbed by where my life was leading me. Still, I followed.

George suggested a Turkish restaurant on 2nd Avenue. It was inviting, it smelled great, and the wine was good, too. If you like rosé at all, then you really should try a Turkish one. Ours was perfect with the delicious food that began to appear on our table. After our initial greeting and polite cheek kisses, George and I hadn't much to say. Ordering dinner is serious business, after all. But with choices out of the way and a little wine and appetizer in our bellies, we began to relax.

"I would have cooked for you, Paul, but I don't think my cooking would bring you much joy. My mother never let me watch her. And the food that emerged from her kitchen was no great shakes. She made a credible brisket. That was about it. I always remember reruns of a vintage comedy routine by the late, great Buddy Hackett, talking about his Jewish mother's cooking. He said he never ate any other food until he went into the army, at which point he thought, *I must be dying. The fire went out!*

"I'm sure you're better than that, George," I said, "but we have so little time together. So, let's use it wisely." We did. After dinner and very good coffee, Paul suggested we stroll to his apartment, maybe only fifteen minutes away. I accepted, as graciously as I could manage while at the same time holding a sense of deep moral failure. My, that sounds Christian. Perhaps it was.

There wouldn't be much sundown relief from the late summer heaviness in the air, but at least there was a slight breeze. We held hands as we headed down to East 72nd Street and then west to Lexington

Avenue. From there it was a straight shot to George's place. I was in no hurry. I was with George, he was holding my hand, and I hadn't yet done anything I'd regret in the morning. As we neared George's building, I suspected that was about to change.

George let us in and said, "Paul, will you come to the bedroom? Will you let me hold you? Your skin against my skin is what I've always wanted most." I agreed. No surprise, there. We stripped and lay together in the evening summer sunlight. George's body was so ... comfortable, I suppose. Except for when he took my left ass cheek in his right hand. I feared I might levitate. We'd had a big dinner, so there would be no aerial feats that night. We savored our union—our time together.

George poured two Scotches. We went to the living room and sat in front of the fireplace, which I could imagine as a glorious place to be on a winter night. Even in the full heat of summer—with good air conditioning, of course—it was quite cozy. "Didn't I meet Maryanne once, at some family event at Columbia?" George asked. "I'm sure your parents were there."

"Good memory," I said. "It's probably the only time they ever came to New York City. Maryanne was sixteen, I guess. Yes, she came with them."

"Very pretty. She looked so much like you, Paul. Same eyes, same hair, same smile. I shouldn't tell you this, but I had a little fantasy about going to bed with both of you at the same time. Good thing fantasies can just stay in Fantasyland."

"I think you remember everything, George," I said. "I thought I was the only one."

"Paul, I don't want to pressure you, but I'd love you to live here with me. There's plenty of room, and there's even an extra bathroom so we wouldn't have to stumble over each other on busy mornings. Please think about it."

"I will, George," I said. "What would your kids think—every other weekend—of their new Uncle Paul? Or would I be the evil stepmother?"

"I enjoy a little drama now and then, Paul, but I'd prefer something simple and direct tonight. Please tell me what you want, and I'll do it."

"If only I knew, George. If only I knew. I know I'm not being very nice. You don't deserve to be dangled. It's just that my emotions are such a tangle these days. I thought my life was chugging along nicely. I thought my relationship with Jason was nearly perfect. He's *entirely* perfect, by the way. And then one day *you* turned up, and I froze like a deer in the headlights."

"This is not a hunt, Paul," George said. "It's a chance for us to make up for lost time. And speaking of time, take all you need. I'm not going anywhere. I'll wait, Paul, even if it takes you years to decide. You're all I want. And I can be a very patient man." I fell into George's arms, and we kissed for a while. It was a lovely ending to a lovely evening. I prepared to head home.

George asked, "Will you let me see Maryanne this week? We have a little history, after all."

"I don't know, George," I said. "I haven't gotten that far yet. She never has much free time when she's in town. I'm sure Clyde will want to cook for her one night. And he'll probably invite Lily and Jason, too. But not me, of course. Clyde's an excellent host. He would never put a guest in an uncomfortable situation. I think that will prove to be a two-Ambien night for me."

"It's not important, but I would like to see her, Paul. Every link to our past is precious to me."

"I promise I'll ask her, George, and I promise I'll tell her about us. She's so smart. Did I tell you what she does? She heads up the AI department for a nonprofit that creates telecommunication systems for developing nations. She got the service gene— and the technology gene. I didn't get either."

"Don't sell yourself short, *Sonnenschein*. You have so much to offer the world. Did I really just call you …?"

"Yes, and I liked it," I said. "George, I still don't understand how we lost what we had. But I'll shut up. It's getting late, and it's a school night, after all. And I have to make some sense of clean sheets and towels for Maryanne. I'll head home. And I'll promise to keep in touch with you."

"And to be very good to yourself?"

"If that's what you want," I said. "I'll try." We embraced. I thanked George for a beautiful evening. One last kiss, and I headed home. One more moment in George's apartment and I might have taken root there. But I extricated myself just in time.

Chapter Seven

Maryanne arrived pretty much on time on Friday evening. I greeted her and carried her bags to the bedroom. "Why am I sleeping here?" she asked.

"Because I said so. And besides, I prefer the couch."

"Paul, how's Jason? *Where's* Jason?"

"I'll explain it later. First, let's get you settled in."

"I hate it when you play the Man of Mystery," Maryanne said as she unpacked a little. "But I'm a woman, after all. So I'm used to waiting patiently."

I reached for Maryanne and embraced her too firmly. I said, "Please don't beat up on me, Annie. I'm not in a very good emotional place."

Maryanne returned my embrace and said, "Okay, Pauly. Give me a minute, and I'll come out and have a nightcap with you."

"Maryanne, you look ... radiant!" I said as I poured cognac for us. "You must be in love. Tell big brother all about it."

"I wish," she said. "But you seem to be the only one who can manage affairs of the heart, Paul. It's not as if Mother and Dad set a great example."

"Please," I said. "I'd slit my wrists if I found myself trapped in a marriage like theirs. Do you see them?"

"Once a month, or so. It's tolerable. They've grown older and smaller, of course. Less formidable. I can drop in for a short visit and then get on with my day. It used to take an emotional toll on me just being in the same room with them. But lately I just let it go."

"You may be on to something about your being a woman. Patience and all. I think it's five years ago that I was last in Buffalo, and that felt like one trip too many."

"Leave it, Paul," Maryanne said. "You've found your method. If you became suddenly attentive there would be no thanks in it. I'll check in on them and do what needs doing. There's no point in both of us being miserable."

"I don't deserve you," I said. "But that's the story of my life. On a happier note, when will you be free to have dinner with me? I'm sure the weekend is super busy."

Yes," she said. "My weekend is all booked up. Clyde invited me for Monday. It didn't sound like you'd be there. What's that about?"

"Yes, well, I have some explaining to do. But first, let's make a schedule."

"Sure. Tuesday I'm having dinner with one of our clients. But Wednesday evening I'm free. And then I have to head home on Thursday morning. I love New York, and I never have enough time here."

"I love *you*," I said. "And no, you never stay long enough. Please save Wednesday for me. I have a couple of ideas. Remember when you came to Columbia with the Folks? Do you remember George?"

"George Adler? He was gorgeous!"

"He's even *better* looking now. And he wants me back."

"Ouch!"

"I ran into him on the street a week and a half ago. He invited me to have dinner with him. And my life has been upside down ever since."

"What about Jason?"

"Exactly. Well, the short version is that I couldn't be honest with Jason. I couldn't open up to him about my memories and my feelings for George. And so he left me."

"Can you get him back?" Maryanne asked.

"I hope so. But first I'd have to tell him the truth. And I don't know, Annie. I don't know what the truth is. I know that I love Jason just as much as I always have. But I also know that I've devoted half my life to loving George. The memories used to be manageable. Actually seeing him again? Quite a different experience. Seismic, I'd call it."

"Poor baby," Maryanne said as she caressed my face. "You have a lot to deal with."

"Clyde knows, of course. But he'd never betray my trust. Jason doesn't know because I couldn't tell him. And Lily doesn't know either, I don't think. So when you see them on Monday, please don't say anything that would be hurtful to Jason. That didn't come out right. But you know what I mean."

"Of course I do," Maryanne said. "I'll be careful."

"Will you see George on Wednesday? He asked specifically for a chance to see you again. He was quite taken with the lithe sixteen-year-old you were back then. I think he'd find the woman even more interesting. And, selfishly, I'd love to get your feedback. I could make a dinner plan for the three of us."

"Sure," Maryanne said. "That sounds nice. Just let me know where I have to be and when."

Bruce K Beck

"Of course," I said. "And now, let's get you to bed, Warrior Woman. I'm sure you have many battles to fight tomorrow." I made sure Maryanne had everything she needed, and then I retired to the living room, where I had already placed some bedding. Fortunately, I was telling the truth—I really did find the sofa very comfortable. I would be fine there. Another splash of cognac and I was ready for sleep.

📖

I slept late on Saturday morning, and then I texted George with a dinner invitation for Wednesday evening. I told him Maryanne would be joining us. I knew he'd be pleased. I also knew that having Maryanne along would afford my heart a little protection from another frontal attack by *George's* heart. Or so I hoped. Everything I did those weeks felt like flying by the seat of my pants.

I hadn't spoken to Clyde in—a week? I texted him, "Will you phone me?" He did. "Bless you, my son," I said. "There will be rewards for you in heaven."

"I'd prefer earthly rewards, but I'll I take what I can get. What's up, Father?"

"Oh, Clyde. I've had three dates now with George, and I still don't know what I'm doing. I feel like such an idiot carrying on like this—at our age! I'd rather take poison than hurt Jason, but I just can't ignore George's twenty-year claim on my heart. What would you do?"

"I would make certain that I didn't get myself into your predicament. But once in, who knows, Pauly? The only important thing is the decision you make.

44

And of course no one can really help you with that. I'll support you, whatever you choose. If you decide to leave Jason, then Lily will never speak to you again. But you knew that. I'm Switzerland, however. You can come to me for your ski holiday whichever partner you choose."

"That's very generous," I said. "But please promise you won't take up yodeling."

"Not a chance."

"Good. Thank you, Clyde. I feel a bit better. Maryanne is looking forward to seeing you on Monday. She's adored you for years and years. I told her as much as I could about what's going on. So she knows to avoid the topic of Paul at dinner."

"I'm looking forward to it," Clyde said. "It will be fun to watch the dynamic between the two ladies. Lily is ... highly competitive. She's accomplished, of course, but her business smarts are quite different from Maryanne's technical brilliance. Jason will be a saint, of course. It should prove to be a most interesting evening."

"Did I ever tell you that Maryanne met George at Columbia? She was sixteen; we were twenty. They both remember the meeting. The three of us are having dinner on Wednesday. George wanted to see her, and I wanted to have her along to help me gain some perspective. Maybe. How's Jason? I miss him so much I can hardly stand it."

"Jason is strong as an ox, of course. He seems to be holding up well. Paul, don't leave him dangling too long. Don't think he'll wait forever. And don't think he couldn't re-partner tomorrow."

"I know, Clyde," I said. "You're absolutely right. I'm doing my best here. Pray for me."

"Yes, well, I'm not so sure about my communications channel with the Old Man these days. But I'll see. Let me know how Wednesday goes."

"I love you, Clyde!" And I was back to being entirely alone.

I was nervous about our Wednesday dinner. I wanted someplace warm and welcoming with great food, of course, but not too dark and romantic. I chose Café d'Alsace, on the Upper East Side, which had long been a favorite of mine. They offered a table for three at 7:00. Perfect.

On Wednesday, Maryanne got to my place—after a busy day, of course—about 6:00. So she had a minute to freshen up and change for dinner. "Annie, thanks again for agreeing to come with me tonight. I don't know how I'd have gotten through it alone."

"Shut up, Paul," she said. "You're spoiling my appetite."

"Quite right, dear." We headed out in silence and took a cab across town. We were a few minutes early. The host seated us. George arrived a minute later. I introduced the two of them, and they greeted each other like old friends. I arranged the seating so George and I were facing each other, with Maryanne between us. I requested a bottle of Gewürztraminer. So far, so good.

We ordered dinner, and then we settled in for a visit. George said, "I was delighted when Paul told me you'd be in town, Maryanne. I remember, of course, how pretty you were all those years ago, and now you've become a beauty."

"You're very skilled at flattery, Mr. Adler," Maryanne said pleasantly. "Most American men make a compliment sound like a put-down. But yours is welcome. Still, I think you should save that for my brother. Paul needs it more than I do these days." I think George and I both blushed.

"Paul knows exactly how much I admire him," George said, "and how I feel about him. But let's let him out from under the microscope. Please tell me about Buffalo. I've never been there, and I have no sense of it."

"Buffalo," Maryanne said. "It's not nearly as grim as most people imagine it. Like so many other cities in this country, if you have a reason to be there, you can build a very satisfying life. We have restaurants and cafés and galleries and colleges and museums and theaters. I love my work. So I *do* have a good reason to be there. And, as Paul knows, it lets me look in on our parents—as little as possible. The winters are rough. But we also have an airport."

"I don't have any plans to travel to Buffalo, but if I do, will you be my tour guide?" George asked.

"With pleasure," she said. The food started to arrive. It was delicious. We ate, we drank, we chattered. It was a lovely evening. Café d'Alsace is one of those places that is so smart about creating an atmosphere of intimacy at each table while at the same time fostering a sense of community with the other guests. It's about the spacing of the tables, of course, the lighting and the careful use of candles, and also about noise levels. I never sensed a single decibel above a contented buzz.

Over coffee and a shared dessert, Maryanne said, "I like you very much, George. I knew I would. But you're disrupting Paul's life. I love Jason, by the way. He's a wonderful man, and he's devoted to Paul. I don't want to see anyone hurt. What do *you* think is going on here?"

George's face looked as dark as I'd ever seen it. He took a moment to gather his thoughts. "Your brother is a very special man, Maryanne. But then you know that," George said. "I've loved him for twenty years. I wasn't certain I'd ever be able to welcome him back into my life. But in the last few weeks I've dared to hope it might be possible. But not if it causes pain. I'll step aside in a heartbeat, if that's what he wants."

"Wasn't that a great meal?" I said. "I'm going to get Maryanne back to my place so she can get some rest before she has to fly in the morning. Thanks for joining us, George. Will you phone me tomorrow?" He said he would, of course, and our dinner ended. I hustled Maryanne into a taxi, and we made the trip to the West Side in silence.

"I think you're angry with me," Maryanne said over a nightcap.

"No, dear. I could never be angry with you. I'm angry with myself for thinking I could thrust you into my drama without consequences. I had no right. I suppose I hoped you'd give me some insight. And you certainly have. I hope I've done some growing up tonight. And I hope I have some adult decisions to report the next time we speak."

Maryanne held me tenderly and said, "Be careful, Pauly. This is for keeps, you know. You're precious to me, Big Brother."

"Not as precious as you are to me, Sis," I said. "I booked your trip to the airport with a car service. They're very good at making sure their clients arrive on time. Get some rest."

What a night! What a week! I slipped between the sheets and never stirred until the alarm jangled me awake.

Chapter Eight

The workday had a surreal feel to it, as if I were performing in an underwater ballet. By noon, I had dried out a bit, I suppose. I ate half a sandwich at my desk. Not very satisfying. George phoned around 1:00. I had asked him to, of course. He thanked me for dinner and said how much he enjoyed being with Maryanne. I hadn't much to say. I asked him if he'd give me the weekend to gather my thoughts—and feelings, of course. He agreed.

George added, "There's going to be a big interfaith conference at the synagogue starting a week from Sunday with a convocation in the big sanctuary. I think you should come. The Diocese will receive invitations for the priests, of course. I'm sure the Bishop will attend. He always shows up for these things. But I'd like you to be there. What do you think?"

"Sounds good. Thank you, George. I was only at Temple Emanu-El once—for a funeral a decade ago—but I found it very impressive. I'd like to see it again. It's as good a place as any for prayers to rise up to Heaven, with or without incense. Keep me posted. Will you phone me next week?" George assured me he would, and our conversation was over.

Clyde phoned me a bit later. "Paul, come for dinner on Sunday night," he said. "I have an idea." I agreed, of course. Clyde's ideas were generally brilliant. Meanwhile, I had the rest of the day to consider, and all day Friday and Saturday. I started to get really hungry, so I buzzed Jeremy:

"What's the best Southern restaurant around here?" I asked. "I've been to Miss Somebody's Spoonbread, or whatever it is. Is that still around?"

"Very much so, Mr. Cornell. They have good food—especially brunch—and it's only a few blocks away, but I know other places as well. Why don't you let me take you out? I have plans for tonight, but I'm free tomorrow night. What do you think?"

"I think that sounds lovely. I'll put myself in your capable hands, as I do every day. Speaking of which, is there anything pressing for the rest of the afternoon? Because I was thinking of heading home."

"You have one phone call, at 2:00. You could take it at home or I can postpone it. That's about it."

"Good," I said. "I'm going to take off. Please forward that call to me. And there's no reason for you to hang out and do busy work, so I think you should leave early, too. As soon as you can. Thanks, Jeremy!"

"Thank *you*, Mr. Cornell. Have a pleasant evening, and I'll see you in the morning."

"Oh, Jeremy, there's going to be a big interfaith prayer event at Temple Emanu-El a week from Sunday. I don't want to intrude on your weekend, but I'd like you to join me if you can."

"Of course, Mr. Cornell. Sounds interesting. Safe home." I took off as soon as I could. The rest of the day was dreary, but the monotony of it was almost comforting. Takeout supper, some CNN, and early to bed.

Friday morning was equally dreary, but the prospect of a good dinner with Jeremy shone like a beacon through the fog. Fortunately, there hadn't been a juicy sex scandal involving the Diocese in decades, and the neighbors in the various parishes were reasonably comfortable with the way we interacted with their communities. There would always be minor skirmishes over our real estate—which is extensive and not subject to the tax rolls, of course—but I always felt privileged to be working for the Episcopal Diocese of New York rather than the Roman Catholic Archdiocese of New York. God bless them, but I wouldn't want to assume their legal headaches.

A bite of lunch at my desk. A few minor fires to extinguish. Nothing too demanding. By 5:00 I was hungry and thirsty, too. "Where are you taking me?" I asked Jeremy.

"You'll see," he said. We finished up and headed out. He led me to a restaurant just a few blocks east of the Cathedral, on West 114th Street, I think. It was busy, welcoming, and comfortable. With a big bar. We started with a Sazerac cocktail. I think I drank one in New Orleans once. But that could be just a fantasy—the cocktail, not my *Mardi Gras* trip to New Orleans with Clyde. That was real enough.

"What should I order?" I asked.

"Your choice," Jeremy said. "Chicken and waffles, if you're in the mood. I always like the cheese grits with grilled shrimp."

"Sold," I said. "The menu says two sides. What should I choose?"

"Not mac & cheese, with the grits," Jeremy said. "I'd go with collards and black-eyed peas, if I were you."

"I can't imagine why you'd want to be me, but I'm happy to take your advice."

"What makes you think the idea of being you isn't appealing?" Jeremy asked. "You're handsome, you're charming, you're bright, you're accomplished. If I had to give up being black—which I have no interest in doing—I'd take your life in an instant, Paul."

"Instead of trading lives, Jeremy, I think we should try to enjoy the ones we have. Is this going to be too much food?"

"Of course," Jeremy said. "I sometimes take the sides home. Save room for dessert, though. The banana pudding is legendary."

"Uncle!" I said. Food began to arrive. It was delicious, as was the house red wine. I loved being with Jeremy. It was all so light and uncomplicated. He seemed so comfortable in his beautiful skin. He accepted our evening together as easily as he ordered food and drink. As easily as he took a breath, released it, and took another. I envied his ease. And I wondered if I could learn something from him about life.

I was aware, after all, that Jeremy had lived through crushing disadvantages by virtue of being born black—and beautiful—in the United States in the late twentieth century. I wondered if I knew anything at all about the legacy of slavery. I wondered if Jim Crow was anything more than an historical concept to me, while across the table from me sat a young man who knew all about both and still bore them with extraordinary grace and poise.

Jeremy said, "That's a great suit, Paul. You always look perfect when you come to the office. A good tailor can present whatever you want the world to see. He can make you invisible. He can make you look like much more than you really are. He can present exactly what you have. Or he can leave a sense of mystery."

"And my tailor?"

"Somewhere between accuracy and mystery, I'm guessing. A good place to be. I'd stay there, if I were you."

"And your tailor?"

"My tailor likes it very much when I suck his big black cock. So he'll give me whatever look I want—cautious for the office and outrageous for my real life. Did you know that careful tailoring can make my ass look exactly like yours? It's true. I'm not saying that you don't have butt beautiful. I'm certain you do. But mine? You won't really be able to appreciate it until I drop these trousers." I didn't gulp, exactly, but I may have blushed a little.

Coffee arrived, and Jeremy said, "Why don't you come to my place, Paul? I put clean sheets on the bed this morning, and I've got some groceries, since I usually make breakfast on Saturday morning. What do you think?"

"I think you're a very nice man, Jeremy. And a very attractive man. But I have too many men in my life as it is."

"I'm not expecting a proposal of marriage, Paul. Just a sleepover. It's not really that complicated. What do you think?"

I did a quick review of my single status, since Jason left me. And I thought, *What do lonely men do? They have sex, of course.* I felt an intense need for it.

In fact, a tingling sensation had started in my crotch as soon as we were seated across from each other at table. And the tingle increased in intensity as the evening went on, to the point that by the time Jeremy asked me over, the tingle became so strong I feared it might be audible. "Yes," I said.

"Good," Jeremy said. "Let's get a check and get out of here." And that's what we did. Jeremy's apartment was only a few blocks away. We were about a block into our trip when a speeding car slowed down just long enough for the guy in the passenger's seat to shout, "Death to nigger lovers!" And then the car sped away. I was rattled. Jeremy let it roll right over his head. He'd heard worse, surely. We quickly continued our walk. I tried to put the incident behind us.

By the time we had arrived and Jeremy had let us in, we were practically panting. And it had nothing to do with being winded by the journey. Jeremy kissed me as soon as he had bolted his door behind us. It was a generous kiss. Warm, passionate. "Why don't you make yourself comfortable while I pour us a glass of wine?"

I liked Jeremy's apartment, very much. It was a large studio with careful use of space. Jeremy's bed was the most important feature in the room, but it doubled as a sofa during the day, with large bolsters and sofa pillows covered in African indigo fabrics that were inviting to the eye and to the hand—rather like their owner. And from the large, open kitchen, Jeremy could survey it all.

He watched me taking it in as he poured wine. I was certain he did. And then he joined me. We sat. We sipped. "I've imagined you here," Jeremy said. "You must have known that."

"I hope I'm not stupid, Jeremy. I've had some imaginings, too. But I've been happily partnered all the time you've worked at the Diocese. So I never thought ...."

"I don't care what changed your mind, Paul," he said. "I'm just glad you're here. I don't think we need any conversation. I'm going to take your clothes off." And that's what he did. His own, too, of course. Shoes and socks take a while, but in a few minutes we faced each other in full birthday.

"Jesus, Jeremy!" I said. "You take my breath away."

"Shut up, Paul," he said. "Kiss me!" I did, of course. Jeremy deftly cleared all the sofa paraphernalia from the bed and pulled down the coverlet. What a romp! Jeremy was aggressive, he was passive, he was assertive, he was receptive. He worshiped my body and encouraged me to worship his. He was a force of nature, really. He was intensely physical while at the same time his soaring energy lent a spiritual element to the proceedings. You've heard people speak of encounters with angels? I suspected I was having one. Still do.

We bounced around Jeremy's bed for a half hour or so, I guess. And then he focused on what he wanted next. Jeremy threw his strong legs over my shoulders and offered me full access to the inner sanctum. I was humbled by the gesture but eager to perform my adoration well and truly. I entered. I studied Jeremy's face, between kisses, in the hope of learning if my worship was acceptable. Jeremy looked blissful. I took that to mean I was maybe getting it right.

Before too much longer there were great spasms and then there was cum everywhere. We both laughed and kissed some more. When I had recovered a bit, I asked, "Did I just go to church? I feel washed clean."

Jeremy laughed heartily and said, "All my sex partners tell me they've had a religious experience. Why should you be different?"

"Do you really want me to sleep over?" I asked. "I do know how to find my way home."

"Of course I want you here," Jeremy said. "Didn't I promise you breakfast?" I relaxed into the plan. We talked for a while and kissed for a while, and then we brushed our teeth and headed for bed. I tend to be a little tense about sleeping in a new bed. Not that night. Jeremy kissed me sweetly, and I conked out.

It was a lovely, lazy Saturday morning. Jeremy sautéed breakfast sausages and sliced apples. He scrambled eggs. He toasted good bread and served it with artisanal butter and peach jam his mother made. Delicious. He also served me New Orleans coffee and chicory, which I hadn't tasted in years. It was a perfect morning feast. We sat at the counter in Jeremy's kitchen, smiled a lot, and enjoyed our breakfast in silence.

When I had eaten a little too much, I put down my napkin, pushed back from the counter, and smiled contentedly. "You're a nice man, Jeremy," I said. "How come you're single?"

Jeremy laughed easily and said, "I can imagine being married to a great guy. But not anytime soon. I'm having too much fun. Imagine—if I had made a commitment along the way, then I'd have missed the chance to make love to you. And I'm not willing to miss chances like that. Not now. If it started to feel hollow, maybe. Meanwhile ...?"

"I think you're on the perfect path, Jeremy. I think you should continue to spread joy to needy men. Like me."

"I thought you had a surplus of men in your life, Paul. Tell me about them."

"Yes, well, Father," I said. "It all started when I was twenty." Jeremy looked skeptical. "No, it's true." I gave him the quick version of my history with George, ending with, "And that's the guy you'll meet at the interfaith convocation a week from Sunday. I'll be interested to get your impression of him. I think he's wildly attractive. I think most people do."

"And?" Jeremy asked.

"Yes, well, I didn't see George for nineteen years. Not until a few weeks ago. And in the meantime, I fell in love with a terrific guy named Jason. He's a personal trainer, so you know he has the body of death. And he has the sweetest nature of any man I've ever met—until I met you, of course."

"Don't change the subject. What's up with Jason?" Jeremy said.

"I couldn't tell him about George. That's it, really. He waited as patiently as he could for me to tell him what was wrong, and I couldn't do it. And so he left me."

"Ouch!" Jeremy said. "Now what?"

"Yes, well, I think Clyde has an idea. He's my best friend. You've met Clyde, I think. My bedrock. He's such a good man. Anyway, I'm hoping to fix things, and soon."

"Meanwhile," Jeremy said, "why don't you come back to bed?"

"Good thinking," I said. And that's what we did. Our second toss, in the morning sunlight, was easier and less urgent than the night before. I held Jeremy close and drank in his essence. The combination of breakfast, coffee, and Jeremy's natural scent—like sweet grass lightly bruised—was a heady mix. I tried to memorize it, suspecting that the experience would never be repeated.

"Thank you for a lovely visit," I said. "I'll give you your life back now, Jeremy."

"Stay as long as you like, Paul," he said. "I'm not going anywhere today."

"I've intruded long enough. I'll head home now."

"An intrusion like this is always welcome," he said. "Always."

"Thanks, Jeremy," I said. "I'll remember that. And I'll remember our time together—very fondly." I pulled on my clothes and went home. I felt relaxed, and I smiled a lot. Being with Jeremy was enough to take the edge off my entire Saturday. I wasn't able to work up even a bit of anxiety until morning.

Chapter Nine

I woke with a start Sunday morning. Surely Clyde had conspired to find me some alone time with Jason. I had to be ready for him. I had to get it right. I owed that much to him—and to me. All the calm I had experienced with Jeremy vanished, leaving me raw emotions and indecision. Not a great combination.

By noon, thanks to deep breathing exercises and a meditation technique I had learned years before from a kindly Tibetan monk, I began to get my brain a bit centered. I was quiet for the rest of the afternoon, and then it was time for me to dress and go to Clyde's. "Jason and Lily will be here in about a half hour," he said. "I'll get her out of here, somehow, so you two can be alone. Do you know what you need to say to him?"

"I do, actually—some of it, anyway. And I'll make up the rest."

"Good. Here's a glass of wine, but don't drink too much!"

"Thank you, Father," I said. "I won't." We sat quietly until the doorbell rang. Clyde sprang into action.

"What's *he* doing here?" Lily hissed.

"Now, Lily, let's remember our manners," Clyde said.

Bruce K Beck

"Come on, Jason. Let's get out of here!"

"*Lily!*" Clyde barked. She froze. "I just realized I didn't buy enough wine for dinner. Come with me, and we'll buy some now. You can help me carry it." Lily agreed, reluctantly, and they were out the door.

"You look good, Paul," Jason said. "I've been worried about you."

"Not nearly as worried as I've been about you, surely," I said. "Jason, will you let me talk to you? I have some things to say that I've never been able to say to you. I hope it isn't too late."

"Speak to me, Paul," he said.

"I met a man in college. His name is George Adler. We were very much in love, and then he had to leave school because of his father's illness. And I never heard from him again. Until I ran into him on East 65th Street a few weeks ago. George asked me to have dinner with him. I accepted. I wanted to tell you, but I couldn't do it. I couldn't tell you I had had an obsessive love for this guy for twenty years and that he had suddenly reappeared. So I lied to you and told you I had a business dinner. I'm deeply ashamed."

"The night you came home drunk," Jason said. "I remember, of course. Why, Paul? Why couldn't you tell me? Is our bond so superficial that you felt you couldn't trust me with the deepest secrets of your heart?"

I started to cry. I was afraid I would. I said, "I don't know, Jason. I also don't know why I've never been able to tell you how much I love you. I do, of course. And I'm telling you now."

"Now what, Paul? I can't go inside your heart."

"You live there," I said.

"Thanks for saying that, Paul, but I think you have a decision to make. How long do you expect me to wait?"

"I know this is lame, Jason, but I'm making progress. Maryanne helped me see how thoroughly George has upended my life."

"Am I the only one who doesn't know about him?" Jason asked.

"Maryanne has always known about George," I said. "She *met* him, twenty years ago. Clyde knows. I confided in him maybe fifteen years ago, when our love affair started to cool. George was probably the reason. No one else." I had a sudden pang, remembering that I had told Jeremy a little of my history. But I quickly classified that omission as a tiny, entirely necessary white lie. And I got on with the business of telling the truth. "I don't know why I didn't tell you about George. I should have told you when we started dating. But I didn't. And then I couldn't. Until tonight."

"Paul, just do what you have to do," Jason said. "I'm not going to stop loving you because you're stringing me along. I'll wait for your decision as long as I can. Please be kind to both of us." I reached for Jason, and he fell into my arms. I hadn't embraced him in so long that I had nearly forgotten how peaceful he made me feel. How whole. I asked Jason for a kiss. He agreed. I was suddenly home for the first time in weeks.

Jason and I were sitting quietly on the sofa when Clyde and Lily returned. Dinner was a bit chilly, but everyone was reasonably well behaved—even Lily. Her eyes shot daggers from time to time. No surprise there. I was prepared to deflect them. Lily and Jason left right after coffee. "So, how did it go?" Clyde asked.

"Jason listened. He understood everything I told him. Of course he understood. He understands *everything*. I feel like such a jerk for letting this all drag on."

"Now what?"

"Exactly." I had no answer. "Thank you, Clyde. I'll never be able to thank you properly for your friendship. I couldn't love you more."

"Save that for your boyfriends, dear," Clyde said. "I know I told you I'm Switzerland, but I'm starting to thaw. I'm starting to think you should grovel at Jason's feet and beg him to come home. It's none of my business, of course, but that's where I'm leaning. Don't mind me." I embraced Clyde and held him for a long while.

Eventually I said, "You're quite right, of course. Don't think I don't know it, Clyde. It's just that I can't bring myself to give up the idea of George—after all these years. Sound familiar? I'm not claiming it's sound mental health. It's just the way it is. I wouldn't blame you if you gave up on me. I've considered giving up on myself."

"Shut up, Paul," Clyde said. "Go home. Get some sleep. Who knows, you might be sane when you wake up in the morning. Stranger things have happened. Call me." I assured him I would. And I headed home to my empty bed.

📖

"Good morning, Mr. Cornell."

"Good morning, Jeremy. How was your week-end?"

"Excellent, thanks. And yours?"

"Quite remarkable, thanks." Another work week began. Jeremy was just as sweet, and hot, and efficient as ever. There were a few small matters that actually required my attention and my expertise. I am a decent attorney, after all. It was gratifying to have some real work to do. I focused on it and stopped feeling sorry for myself for a couple of hours.

I phoned Clyde to thank him for dinner—and all the rest of his friendship. "Any overnight miracles in the mental health department?" he asked.

"None, unfortunately," I said. "But the therapy has begun, Doctor."

"Good," he said. "Don't be a slacker. Take your medicine, Paul. Get better."

"Will do, Doc," I said. An hour later George phoned. I had asked him to, of course.

"I've missed you. Terribly," George said.

"I've missed you, too," I said. It was the truth.

"Will you have dinner with me in the next few days? I'd like that."

"Yes, George," I said. "Why don't we meet after work tomorrow?"

"Sounds great. Choose a place. I don't really care what we eat. I like everything. And I like *you* best of all."

"I'll come up with something and text you," I said. "Thanks for calling, George." I *was* grateful, of course. But I was also mildly disgusted with myself for needing him so.

"Don't forget the convocation on Sunday."

Bruce K Beck

"I wouldn't," I said. "I've asked my secretary to come along. Is that okay? You'll like Jeremy. He's a sweetheart. And hot, too."

"If you like him, I'm sure I will, too. Of course. Bring him along. Until tomorrow, then." And the call was over.

▥

I'm reasonably resourceful, so I was able to dream up a dinner scenario for George and me for the following night. It had to be casual, not what you'd call romantic, and not too close to George's apartment. I decided on Chinatown and a restaurant that's famous for noodles and also for soft-shell crab, in season. And it was high season. And no one had ever accused the place of being romantic.

George was a good sport, naturally. We got a tiny table after a very short wait on the Bowery. We drank Tsingtao beer and ate too many crispy soft-shell crabs. They were delicious. *George* was delicious. It didn't matter the setting. If we had brown-bagged it on the Staten Island Ferry, he'd have been just as easy and fun. That was part of what made my choice so difficult. I knew by our second date that George could make me happy—effortlessly—for the rest of my life.

But, even ignoring the future, there were immediate choices to make. And I don't mean just the 6 train or a taxi. George invited me back to his apartment, as I knew he would. I accepted his invitation (as I knew I would? Probably). Taxi. Two choices made. We traveled uptown mostly in silence. Taxis have such bad shocks these days that there's not

64

much point in conversation while bouncing along New York City streets.

George welcomed me into his apartment. Again. I felt guilty about being there. Again. But when he kissed me, *most* of my qualms melted away. Again. "George, this is crazy," I said.

"I think it's great," he said. "I've loved you for twenty years, Paul, and I'll go on loving you for the rest of my life, whatever you decide." George led me to his bedroom. No surprise there. We stripped. I melted into George's arms. We sank into his bed and made love to each other gently, quietly, deliberately. I loved George's skin against mine, his kisses that mirrored the openness of mine, his attention to detail. I loved his dick, especially. It's a perfect size—straight and white with delicate blue veining. The head is generous and flawlessly sculpted, begging attention—worship, really. I did my best to honor it.

When we were sated, we lay together for a while in the soft glow of twilight. It seemed cruel—to both of us—for me to rise and dress and prepare to leave George's comfy nest. And yet that really was the only option. We didn't dwell on it. As I prepared to leave, George embraced me and said, "I meant what I said at dinner last week. I never wanted to cause pain. If I can bring you pure joy, then I'm yours. If not, then I'm history."

I squeezed George and resisted the urge to cry. "I'm not a broken record," I said, "though I know I sound like one. I need time." His embrace assured me he had accepted my terms.

As I prepared to leave, George said, "The service on Sunday starts at 6:00. Meet me at the side door—the museum entrance—at 5:45. I reserved three seats for us up front, and I'll sneak us in the back way."

"Thanks, George," I said. And then I shut up and headed home.

Chapter Ten

Most of the week felt like floating, except for the part that felt like being under water. I slogged through both conditions and got on with it. Jeremy was perfect, as always. He insulated my work life from all the nonsense and office politics that invade even well-run ventures. He presented me the work that needed doing, while at the same time he ran interference on the bullshit that can so easily derail the work train.

On Thursday I asked Jeremy to have lunch with me at a little coffee shop near the office. He accepted. We broke free of our restraints—while keeping our ties and jackets on, of course—and headed out into the sunlight. Leaving the office always made me feel like a child who's been let out of the house after the rain. Law school, indeed. What was I thinking? And yet, I did it. And I did it well.

"What's happening on the romantic front?" Jeremy asked me over chopped salads.

"Too much and not enough," I said. "I wish I had your powers of perception, Jeremy. You seem to know exactly what you want. You go after it. You get it. And then you move on."

Jeremy laughed his silvery laugh and said, "So you have me all figured out, Paul. What if I told you I'd like to continue having Friday night dinner dates and Saturday morning breakfasts with you? I'm not saying that I do, but just suppose. How would that sit in your neat little white world?"

"It would sit quite comfortably, indeed, Jeremy, if I had the purity of heart for it. I'm not talking about good old American racism. I mostly gave that up when I was a child, I think. I hope. Please correct me if I'm wrong. Differences don't interest me, except what I can learn from them. What I *am* talking about is the space in my heart that already belongs to two wonderful men. There isn't room for another wonderful man, as much as I might wish there were."

"Reasonable answer," Jeremy said. "And there I thought the handsome white attorney needed my help."

"I need your help every day, Jeremy, and you know it. Don't be coy."

"*Touché*," Jeremy said. "What are you going to do about those two wonderful men who occupy your heart so totally there isn't even a little corner for me?"

"There has always been a corner for you, Jeremy," I said. "And you know it. I wouldn't have accepted your offer of a sleepover if I didn't admire you. Love you." I started to say something about being too old to bounce from bed to bed, but I thought better of that. Instead, I said, "I'm asking you for the same patience I ask of others in my life. I'm trying to make sense of it all."

"Of course you are," Jeremy said. "But remember you're always welcome at *chez Jérémie*. Even on short notice. As long as you don't mind another guy in bed with us."

"It's been a while," I said. "But I'm sure it would come right back to me. Only one other man? That's hardly group sex."

"You make me blush, Counselor," He said. "Perhaps I've misjudged your tastes."

"Don't," I said. "I'll try to keep things interesting. Just because I'm often on the verge of nodding off at my desk, we can't have that sort of behavior from you."

"Thanks, Boss," he said. "What's the story for Sunday evening?"

"Yes," I said. "I'm sure you've seen Temple Emanu-El on 65th and 5th. There's a stop on the Central Park transverse bus right across 65th Street. George asked us to meet him at 5:45 at the side door. It says Museum something or other. It should be easy to find. You've seen the building, haven't you?"

"Only from the bus," Jeremy said. "It's massive!"

"George is going to sneak us in to one of the front rows. Wait till you see the sanctuary. Have some important prayers ready."

"Always," Jeremy said. "Even though God lives everywhere, he shows his face more clearly in spiritual places, I always thought."

"Something else we have in common," I said. "So, on Sunday evening, don't be late! What am I saying? You've never been late for anything, Jeremy. I probably meant to say that I intend to be a little early. Actually, we could meet for a drink at 5:00."

"Perfect!" Jeremy said. "That way even *you* can't be late for church." We made our plans. And we got through the rest of the week.

Bruce K Beck

There's a restaurant space on 65th just east of Madison, on the north side of the street, that used to be so chic that it had no name and no phone number. It worked for the owners for years. The current occupant is a little more welcoming. They call it a brasserie. That's fine with me. Jeremy and I were only in the market for a glass of wine and perhaps a tiny bite of steak tartare before our church adventure. Perfect. I never liked praying on an empty stomach.

George greeted us at the side door of Temple Emanu-El at 5:45, as promised. I introduced him to Jeremy, and they greeted each other like old friends. So far, so good. George led us to a back stairway that took us to what would have been the choir loft in a Christian church. Not that Emanu-El hadn't adopted various features of Christian worship traditions in the last century. I learned in school that the German Reform movement lost its taste for segregating the sexes and forbidding orchestral music. They had an organ! And a choir! I wasn't certain where the music would come from until the organ rang out and I could trace the source to the organ and choir loft in the back, above the front door.

George navigated us to the second pew, house right. Perfect sight lines. The United Nations of Faiths began to file into the great vaulting sanctuary. There were bishops and archbishops and patriarchs and imams and rabbis—Reformed, Conservative, Orthodox. There were priests and nuns and preachers and monks and a dazzling array of other religious beings. Those who would be speaking made their way to chairs behind the podium, while the others took their places in the pews.

The head rabbi at Emanu-El was the master of ceremonies, naturally. As he headed to the podium, assistants from all faiths followed him up the center aisle and then fanned out all around the sanctuary, censing the space from everywhere at once. I noted a few Eastern Orthodox celebrants with their great robes and hats and beards; someone from our Diocese looking obviously Episcopalian; a junior from the (R.C.) Archdiocese whom I'd seen before and remembered because he was so cute. There was a Buddhist monk in saffron robes, a Shinto priest, a Sikh with a purple turban and huge dark eyes, and a Navajo medicine man with some amazing turquoise jewelry who was wielding a sage smudgestick. A pretty young woman with classic Mayan features carried a tin animal whose head was topped with a small dish containing a few smoldering lumps of copal. There was a celebrant from Africa, swinging his brass censer and looking splendid in blue-black skin and snow-white robes.

Modern Judaism has lost its taste for incense, mostly. But I'll bet they could get it back without too much prodding. Think frankincense and myrrh. I was half kidding when I told George that the sanctuary at Emanu-El was as good a place as any for prayers to rise up to heaven on clouds of incense. And there it was, happening. Heady stuff. Like nothing I've experienced, before or since. The organ finished the processional, and the rabbi began to speak. His words, amplified by a remarkable sound system, pierced the incense fog that hung in the air. Did he start with "Dearly beloved"? Surely it was something like that, but don't quote me. I tend to have a short attention span when it comes to liturgy.

Bruce K Beck

Fortunately, the service had much to recommend it, starting with readings from the Book of Psalms. You can't go far wrong with Psalms—something for just about everyone. The rabbi passed off the podium to the Archbishop (the Roman Catholic one, that is), and the relay had begun. Isn't it amazing how when you assemble a bunch of religious leaders, everyone talks about peace and love? The Qu'ran is filled with it, by the way. Easy to quote. Religious tolerance and brotherly—and sometimes even sisterly—love are always at the fore.

Now, if someone had said, "We embrace our gay brothers and sisters," that would have seemed newsworthy. No one did, of course, although a rabbi got close. She stopped just short of saying something incendiary. So that pretty much retired the topic of Tolerance for the day. Tolerance of our differences, that is. Those men talk a blue streak about religious tolerance.

Even though I was sometimes disappointed with the message, I was pleased to be sitting in a sanctuary that is endlessly fascinating visually. To the glory of God, of course. I knew it was designed so that the thick masonry exterior walls bear all the weight of the great vaulted ceiling without a single column in sight to mar the soaring openness of the space. The fact that I sort of know how they did it does nothing to detract from the majesty of the result.

I can generally handle prayer—whatever the language—for an hour or so. After that, I become restless. I tried to be a good sport, for George's sake, and for Jeremy's. Just when I thought my ass would go numb, we stood to sing a hymn. Hallelujah! I always thought that was an inspired way to keep parishioners awake. I started to imagine having sex with all the best-looking men in the room. Individually and collectively. It helped. The benediction was a great soup of blessings worthy of the Tower of Babel.

And then the service was over. As we filed out of the sanctuary and into the last of the late summer sunlight, I became quite aware of the concrete barricades—disguised as flower boxes—that lined the avenue and the side street. I knew they were there, of course. I remembered when 9/11 forced many houses of worship to protect themselves from drive-in terror. George and I were still at Columbia at the time. We were so far uptown that we could scarcely see—or smell—the gray smoke of ruin that blanketed downtown, not to mention the dust. We knew, though. We knew that life would never be quite the same.

And yet I hadn't thought of that disaster so keenly in years. Not until we stepped onto the porch of Temple Emanu-El and the "flower boxes" became just as visible as the security guards. The crowd began to thin. The goodbyes were heartfelt and physical. What a peaceable kingdom! George had a few things to attend to. He asked Jeremy and me to wait for him. We spoke to one of our favorite priests from the Diocese.

When George returned, there were still many dozens of us gathered in front of the synagogue. I was embracing George and thanking him for the invitation when suddenly all hell broke loose, and the guards shouted, "Get down!" Jeremy shoved me into George, and we both toppled over, but not before I saw a black SUV driving slowly by while two shooters sprayed the crowd with bullets.

We waited for the "all clear." At least I was in George's arms. The guards tried to quiet the shouts. I heard a great thud. It felt like an eternity, but it was probably only a few minutes until the security staff allowed us to spring into action. Suddenly there were congregants fleeing and paramedics appearing on the scene. Cops and sirens everywhere. How many dead? Who knew? How many wounded? Who knew? George and Jeremy and I tried to be useful. We tried to comfort those who were bloodied or distraught.

The guards had taken out the driver of the SUV, while we were down, and it had crashed into the building across the street. That was the thud I heard. The shooters had fled on foot, apparently, with police in hot pursuit. It was what I'd imagined a war zone to be like. I shuddered at the horror of it. Other than that, I assumed I was unscathed until Jeremy said, "Paul, you're bleeding. Let's get your jacket off." And then everything went black.

It was around 9:00 the next morning, I think, when I woke from the sedation that had kept me nearly comatose through the night. As I slipped gradually into consciousness, I became keenly aware of the discomfort in my left shoulder, the IV in my right arm, and the catheter they had shoved up my dick—_after_ I conked out, mercifully. I was also keenly aware of Jeremy and George, who were sitting on either side of the bed, holding my hands.

"You gave us quite a fright, Pauly," George said. "It took the Emergency staff a little time to figure out how much blood you had lost and what it would take to patch you up. The doctor will tell you all about it when he makes his rounds, I'm sure. How do you feel?"

"Pretty much the way I look, I guess. Have you two been here all night?"

"I called Clyde from your phone as soon as they stabilized you," Jeremy said. "He had already seen the incident on the news, so he was frantic. I got a little bossy with him. I hope he forgives me. I insisted he stay home. I told him George and I would be with you through the night, while you slept, and that he could maybe relieve us late morning. I knew Clyde would know who else to call."

"Thanks, Jeremy," I said. "You guys thought of everything. What a kick in the teeth! I have no sense of the damage to my shoulder. But there's no point in thinking about that now, before I've talked to the doctor. What the fuck happened?"

George and Jeremy filled me in on how they had both jumped into the ambulance with me. I had some vague memory of cycling in and out of con-sciousness—mostly out—until we got to New York Hospital. Once the EMS people had slid the gurney out of the ambulance and wheeled me into the ER, I mostly gave in to shock and stopped fighting to stay awake.

"What's the damage at Temple Emanu-El?" I asked.

"We've heard five dead and twelve injured," Jer-emy said. "But who knows what the final tally will be. If you're asking about the building, George says it's sound with a bit of cosmetic damage that'll be easily repaired."

"A white supremacist group took credit for the event, apparently," George said. "But it's probably too soon to be certain about any of this. You need to rest and regain your strength, Paul. There's no point in dealing with the past just now." He was right, of course. The fact that there appeared to be a future in sight was about as much as I could handle that strange Monday morning.

Clyde and Jason arrived about 10:00. Jeremy recognized Clyde from their meeting, so he started the introductions. It was all perfectly ordinary until I looked up and saw George and Jason shaking hands. Now that was bizarre. And yet it seemed mi-nor, considering the other events of the last twelve hours. Jeremy and George both looked exhausted, as well as unshaven and unkempt and quite beautiful. "Get out of here, you two," I said. "The next shift of nurses has arrived." I couldn't tell them how grateful I was for their loving care. So I didn't try. They knew. I started to say something to Jeremy about the office, but I was still too groggy to make much sense, so I just said, "You'll know what to do."

Jeremy said, "We'll bring you some supper, so you don't have to face hospital food." He squeezed my hand, and then they both headed out, presumably to someplace that included breakfast and some well-deserved sleep.

"Maryanne's flight gets into LaGuardia around noon," Clyde said. "I told Lily to pick her up. What's the point in keeping a car in the City if you don't help your friends? She got the message. So they should be here one-ish."

"Thank you, Clyde, but you're making a big deal of this," I said.

"It isn't every day that my best friend takes a slug just above his heart, so I'd call it a big deal. A fucking big deal. So don't mess with me, young man. You're in no position to be calling the shots—I wish I hadn't said that," Clyde said. "I need to head to the cafeteria for some coffee. I'll be back in a while. I'm sure you and Jason can think of something to talk about."

Jason and I hadn't been alone together since Clyde's dinner party. That was only a week before. It felt like months. We were *nearly* alone, except for monitoring equipment and the occasional visit from a nurse on some mission or other. Jason said, "Pauly, you've had me so worried. The thought of losing you.... I don't want to live without you, Paul. I'm moving home this evening after George and

Jeremy come back to spell us. I want to be there to take care of you when they send you home."

"I'm hardly an invalid, Jason," I said. "You don't have to disrupt your life on my account."

"Hush, Paul," he said. "I'm going to take care of you, so all you have to do is focus on getting strong." And, naturally, I didn't have the strength to argue with him. So I accepted his plans for his life and mine. "I like George, by the way," Jason said. "Of course you fell in love with him. He's handsome, he's kind. And he obviously worships you—we have that in common." I started to weep softly. "I think we could be good friends, George and I, under other circumstances." We were quiet for a while.

Clyde returned with coffee for both of us. I was not in much shape to feed myself, but Jason held my head and brought the cup to my lips so I could have a swallow or two. It was hospital coffee, and yet it tasted wonderful. Dr. Shapiro walked into my room about noon. I was pleased to be getting some information. I was also nervous, of course, about what I was about to hear.

"You're a lucky man, Mr. Cornell. You've probably heard this on cop shows, but it happens to be true in your case: If the bullet had entered a quarter-inch lower, it would have pierced the aorta. And you'd be in a body bag now instead of in this bed. We're pleased to have you among the living."

"Thanks, Doc," I said. "I'm pleased to be on this side, too. What can you tell me about my shoulder?"

"Yes, well, don't let anyone fool you," he said. "There's no such thing as a simple gunshot wound. After we surveyed the damage we started to clean you up, inside and out. We had to repair some veins and arteries, reattach muscles and connective tissue, and remove bone fragments. We stapled a bone break to stabilize it and speed the recovery. Your shoulder—just as it is today—should heal nicely. In a few months. If it doesn't, we'll have to go back in and see what we missed. We don't anticipate any issues like that, but you never know."

"Thanks for the explanation, Doc," I said. "I was wondering—can you remove the IV? It makes me a little queasy looking at it."

"Sorry, Mr. Cornell," he said. "We have to keep you hydrated, and the IV is the ideal way to administer certain medications. Most patients like our nighttime sleep cocktail, by the way. But that brings me to your next question. The answer is, two more days, I think. Wounds and surgeries are notorious for heating up on the third day. At the first hint of fever, we'll start an antibiotic drip immediately. If we can pass that threshold without incident, and if everything else goes well, then I'll send you home the following morning."

"How about the catheter?" I asked. "I'm feeling quite attached to it, but I'm still willing to give it up."

"We'll take it out this afternoon, if you don't mind," Dr. Shapiro said. "I want you to move around a little. We'll tape your left arm to your body to immobilize the shoulder. Then you can stand up and walk to the toilet, as long as you wheel the IV with you. Tomorrow I want you to walk up and down the hall to get a little exercise. But let's take it gradually."

When the consultation seemed over, I said to Dr. Shapiro, "I'm super hungry."

"That's a good sign."

"Maybe Jason could run over to Pret A Manger for a tuna sandwich. I think I could face half of one, anyway. What do you think, Doc?"

"I think you should eat whatever you want, just not too much of it. They'll bring you an in-house menu. I've eaten worse."

"When will I see you again?" I asked the doctor.

"Tomorrow, on my rounds. About the same time. But if you have any concerns before then, just ask a nurse. They know how to reach me. I don't anticipate you'll have a lot of pain issues—as long as you don't try to practice your left-handed serve. But it's our job to keep you comfortable. If there's anything you need, just ask." And he was on his way. I wasn't certain how to feel about my shoulder. I tried to lift my arm once, and once was enough.

"Let me get that sandwich," Jason said. "What do you want, Clyde?"

"Surprise me," Clyde said. And Jason headed out on his errand. I watched him leaving the room and thought how completely I loved him. And how much I needed him—now more than ever. That frightened me, really. Neediness. How could I let Jason give up his life and his glorious youth to take care of me? No, surely it was wrong. And yet, my condition was temporary, wasn't it?

Clyde said, "You're starting to look more like yourself, dear. That's a good sign. Do you want me to remove the catheter? I do know my way around your dick, after all."

"Very kind," I said, "but let's let a medical expert attend to it, instead of a dick expert." I started to ask Clyde what he had told Maryanne, but I realized he had said exactly what she needed to hear and nothing more. And she'd hear the rest soon enough.

Jason returned promptly with the WASPy treat I had requested. Half a tuna sandwich tasted ambrosial to me.

When the girls arrived, Maryanne sat carefully on the edge of the bed and asked me how close she could get and how physical. I assured her I was not fragile, as long as she avoided my left shoulder. "Pauly, this is crazy," she said. "You're supposed to be the sensible one in the family." She put her hand on my cheek and looked into my eyes, no doubt trying to discern the extent of my injuries.

"The doctor says he'll release me on Thursday morning, most likely, and I'll make a full recovery. It was sweet of you to come, darling, but it really wasn't necessary."

"Shut up, Paul," she said. "You thought I was going to hang out in Buffalo while you're going through this? Forget it. We're not much of a family, but *you* and *I* know how to behave, I hope."

Lily sat on the opposite edge of the bed, took my hand, and said, "Everyone knows you're a drama queen, but really, Paul. This is excessive." She kissed me lightly. "Please stay out of trouble from now on."

"Promise," I said. "Thank you for being kind to Maryanne."

"Nonsense," she said. "That's what fellow Warrior Women are for. I'm going to drive Maryanne to Clyde's so she can settle into his guest room. Should we come back around dinnertime?"

"Thanks, Lil, but too many people are rearranging their lives around my little upset. George and Jeremy are going to bring me some supper—oh, you haven't met them." I said. "Well, it doesn't matter now. Jase, please go with them. Thank you, Lily, for looking after the two people I love most in this world. The staff is going to get me up so I can hobble to the john, as soon as you guys leave. Clyde promised to help. I doubt the rest of you want to watch. Especially the part about removing the catheter. It won't be pretty."

Jason came over to the right side of the bed and held me as much as possible without disturbing my left shoulder or dislodging the IV in my right arm. He kissed me, and said, "Pauly, I'm staying."

"Please do as I ask," I said, quietly. "You've brought me the best possible medicine, Jason, and that's enough for one day. I want you strong and healthy. I want you to live your life. Will you bring me some breakfast?" I called to Maryanne and asked, "Will you come with Jason in the morning and bring me something wickedly caloric? I expect to be ravenous by 8:00, anyway."

Maryanne assured me she and Jason would return in the morning, and then the three of them headed out, reluctantly. I said to Clyde, "Show time!" He rang for a nurse.

Chapter Twelve

Clyde and I navigated the afternoon's activities.   We watched while the nurse removed my catheter. Creepy. We got me up and hobbling to the john. The change of scenery was welcome. Clyde sponged me off. I made a mental note to ask the doctor how long it would take before I could have a proper shower. I had to ask Clyde to brush my teeth, because I couldn't figure a way to manage it myself. Clean teeth can feel like a new lease on life, I learned.

I sat in a chair for a few minutes while a very cute orderly redid my bed. Great ass. Nice smile, too. The sensation in my groin told me I must be on the mend. So that was how my new normal began— slowly, quietly. Clyde insisted on staying until the boys arrived with my dinner. I protested loudly, and yet I loved having Clyde with me. "Darling, you can't keep hanging out here. You must have work to do," I said.

"You know publishing, dear. Nothing much happens on schedule. And besides, there's not a single book I'm editing that's half as important as you are. So, relax and enjoy the service. It won't last forever. I liked seeing the boys this morning," Clyde said. "George is very much as I pictured him. No surprises there. But Jeremy! Did he tell you how he called the shots last night? Sorry, there I go again.   I remembered that Jeremy is cute, and I knew he's efficient, but I had no idea you had yet another conquest."

"Don't be silly," I said. "Just because Jeremy and I had dinner together once and then went to his place and fucked our brains out, it doesn't mean a thing. Guy stuff. Needs. Nothing more."

"Uh-huh. Tell that to someone who's buying it," Clyde said. "I can spot love at twenty paces. And Jeremy's got a bad case. Let him down easy, dear. You owe him that." I didn't feel much like a heartbreaker—at any point in my life, but especially as I lay there in a hospital gown amid tubes and monitors. But I listened to what Clyde told me—as I always did—and resolved to be more careful in the future.

Jeremy and George showed up about 7:00, as promised, bearing a huge shopping bag full of goodies. George opened a bottle of red wine and poured a little all around. We talked and laughed, and I imagined what fun it would be if the four of us had dinner together in some normal setting. No, five of us—Jason needed to be there, too. No, six of us—Clyde should be there with his new squeeze. I resolved to work on it, somehow, since Clyde had been inactive on the romance front for far too long. And with so much to offer! Hmmm.

Clyde declined our dinner invitation and said good night to all of us. I couldn't manage much of an embrace, but my thanks were heartfelt. He headed home. Jeremy reached into the bag and produced some fried chicken wings first thing. "It was either that or gefilte fish," George said. "We decided on fried chicken." I remembered that Col. Sanders always said the best part of the chicken is the middle wing joint. He was right, of course. I always liked wings. We munched, we sipped, we smiled a lot.

"How are things at the Diocese?" I asked Jeremy.

"Oh, you know. There hasn't been this much excitement since Father Gerald was discovered in his office, jerking off on a picture of St. Sebastian. The Bishop wanted to know the hospital and your room number. I told them no visitors, but that you welcome their prayers. How's that?"

"Perfect," I said. "You were always better at religious bullshit than I am. Why didn't you take up the cloth, Jeremy? I've always wondered about that."

"Well, Paul, I didn't grow up in a small-town Southern AME church for nothing. I know how to play the game. And yes, I considered the ministry. But when it came time to get serious about it, I just couldn't make the commitment. I couldn't agree to a lifetime of selfless devotion. I feel closest to God when I'm sucking cock. I experience the miracle of life and love most fully when I'm in another man's arms. Organized religions mostly frown on that sort of thing."

"Maybe we should start our own," George said. "I know I could write bylaws that would put the Talmud to shame. What shall we call it, our new religion?"

"How about The Brotherhood?" I said. "And lesbians can have their Sisterhood—I think they already do. And we can all get together once a month to pray for growth and change in the world. I like it. Sign me up. I've never been a charter member before."

"George and I will draft the necessary documents tomorrow," Jeremy said. "Meanwhile, isn't it time for you to get some of that lovely drug-induced shut-eye?" It was, of course. The guys prepared to leave. Jeremy kissed me and said, "Sleep well, Saint Paul."

"That one's taken," I said. "We'll have to come up with something else. My middle name is Alexander. What do you think?"

"I think it's perfect, Saint Alex," George said. "Get some rest, my little holy man." George kissed me sweetly, on my lips and on my forehead, and they were gone. I got myself up, carefully, and wheeled my paraphernalia to the john for a pre-sleep pee. I was getting good at it. And then I rang for a nurse, who showed up promptly with a tray of medications. She gave me a couple of pills to swallow. I took them, obediently, without even asking what they were.

I said, "How about your famous sleepy-time brew?" She smiled and introduced a fat hypodermic into the valve on my IV. Sweet blindness began to flow all over me. I only had time to think of how comfortable George and Jeremy seemed with each other before sleep claimed me.

I was ravenous in the morning, as I had pre-dicted. I got up, carefully, and rolled my IV stand with me to the john. I had never considered what a pleasure it is to take a real piss, unassisted by probes and tubes and bottles. Yes, pee took on a new reverence for me. I had never been much of a golden shower boy. That might change. Lots of things might change.

Maryanne and Jason were both like rays of sun-shine when they arrived, armed with croissants and marmalade and smoked-salmon sandwiches. They even brought a thermos of very good coffee with lots of hot milk in it—just what I like best for breakfast. I said to them, "I felt like shit until you two arrived. Now, I want to go dancing!"

"Well, Twinkle Toes, maybe that should wait until tomorrow," Maryanne said. "But I'm glad you're feeling better. You look better, too. Yesterday's death pallor has lifted entirely."

"Good news," I said. Jason snuggled up against my right side, as much as possible. I put my arm around him, as much as possible. "You're the best-feeling thing God ever created," I said. "Don't get me started on your virtues, Jason," I said as I tousled his hair. "Not this morning. But just let me name them—maybe one a day—for the next century or so."

"Granted," he said. "Why don't we go to the TV room? You haven't seen NY1 morning news lately. It might do you good to see what's happening in the world. We'll have you back here by noon, for sure."

"Excellent idea," I said. The two of them helped me up, and we headed down the hall. I wondered how I'd feel about *not* wheeling an IV stand with me everywhere I went, once it was history. I decided I'd adjust to the loss quite easily. I said to Maryanne, "So tell me, Sis, what are your plans for this week? If you haven't scheduled at least two important meetings in the next few days, then I'll insist you fly home this afternoon."

"Not to worry, Big Brother," she said. "I made a last-minute date for this afternoon with our Israeli associates. And tomorrow I'm seeing a group of scientists who are working on software for 3-D printing of silicon chips. Fun stuff. Want to come along?"

"Love to," I said, "but I doubt they'd welcome some guy in a hospital gown wheeling his own IV. Better go without me."

"If you insist. Paul, unless you're planning to grow a beard, I think you should ask Jason to shave you today. You're getting a bit scruffy. It's cute, but even so....

"Beard, I think. I haven't tried to grow one since college. I'll ask Jason to shape it a little. Maryanne, I miss you so much when you're not in town. Won't you move to New York? Please?"

"Not now, Pauly. But some day. Meanwhile, just let Jason take care of you."

"I'm putty in his hands."

"Good." We watched the news, which was even scarier than my recent ordeal, of course. And then we headed back to my room. Doctor Shapiro made his rounds at noontime, as promised, with a nurse in his wake. "If you don't mind sitting up, Mr. Cornell, I'd like to take a look at the wounds. Just to make sure everything is as it should be." He looked at Maryanne and Jason as if they were intruders in the room, so I said, "Why don't you two go to the gift shop or something—so Dr. Shapiro and I can be alone," I added suggestively.

The doctor helped me sit up and move to the side of the bed. He opened my gown and began to undo the bandages. I wasn't in any particular discomfort, but I was certainly nervous. "Uh-huh, uh-huh. Nurse Lopez, would you rebandage Mr. Cornell's shoulder, please?" She did, of course. "I like how the wounds are healing—the entry and the exit. You're obviously a healthy man, Mr. Cornell. Let's keep it that way. I told you yesterday to expect a full recovery—surgically—in the next few weeks. But restoring flexibility and strength will be a slow process. You'll probably need some physical therapy." I didn't bother to tell him I had a live-in trainer to recondition my poor, broken body.

"I may not have told you yesterday, but you can expect some numbness throughout the area. It's typical after tissue trauma. The nerves will repair themselves gradually. You're lucky the injury is so close to your heart. That's where the healing is fastest. Don't ever get a busted foot. Takes forever to heal. What kind of aftercare did you arrange?"

"Have you got a minute, Doc?"

"One," he said.

I phoned Jason and asked them to return to my room. I introduced everyone and then said to Maryanne, "Go to work, dear." She kissed me and left us. I said to Dr. Shapiro, indicating Jason, "My caregiver."

Dr. Shapiro smiled and said, "Monitoring his temperature will be the most important thing in the next few days. Every four hours, at least. At the first sign of fever—even one degree—it's back here for an IV antibiotic. That and changing the dressings daily. And making certain he drinks lots of water. Are you okay with that kind of responsibility, Mr. Novak?"

"I am, Doctor," Jason said. "I'm a certified physical therapist as well as a personal trainer. So I'm nearly a medical worker."

"You're very much a medical worker, Mr. Novak. Thank you for your service. I think we can send Mr. Cornell home in the morning. As much as we'll miss him, I think he'll recuperate faster at home than here. Nurse Lopez, do we still have that aftercare brochure at the nurses' station?" She indicated that they did. "Good. Please get them one. It should explain things, Mr. Novak. But don't hesitate to phone if you have any questions. And please get him back here on Tuesday—no, make it Wednesday—for the stitches. If they come out earlier it reduces scarring, but I'm more interested in strength, since it's the shoulder. Good day, gentlemen."

Doctor Shapiro swept out of the room just as suddenly as he had swept in. "Tomorrow morning," I said to Jason. "Will that give you enough time to clear out all the tricks?"

"I hope so, Pauly. I'll do my best."

"See that you do, young man," I said. "Have I told you today how much I love you?"

"No, but the day is still young," Jason said. "Rather like us." I felt flattered that Jason included me in the young category. But then I realized I *was* young, and growing younger by the hour. "Could you help me brush my teeth?" I asked Jason. "This fucking IV makes everything difficult." He did, of course. And afterward, I held Jason as closely as I could and kissed him deeply. "Do you have any idea how much I've missed that?" I asked him.

"I do," he said. It was that kind of afternoon. We kissed a lot. We took a nap. Together. With Jason's head on my right shoulder. We walked down the hall and watched some TV. We took another nap. We were inseparable. I couldn't bear to ask Jason to leave as dinnertime approached. He was happy to stay. I phoned Jeremy, who assured me they were bringing plenty of food. And then I left the whole evening to the care of the gods who arrange these things. Way above my pay grade.

Chapter Thirteen

Actually heading home was even better than my dream version of it. Losing the IV was the first, finest step toward my emancipation. And then everything started to fall into place. My shoulder was still pretty much immobile until the orderly (the cute one with the great ass and the great smile) removed the tape that strapped my arm to my body. I was a little nervous about the state my armpit might be in, once it was liberated. A lateral raise was still impossible, but I managed a very slight forward raise. No horrible fumes escaped.

Jason laughed at me and said, "Pauly, you've been using an antiperspirant for years. The effects linger for days, even when you're not applying it. Underarm odor is a thing of the past—for healthy people who can afford cosmetics, anyway. Maybe we should both go natural. What do you think?"

"I think I could take up residence in your armpits, given half a chance. Maybe I could get dual citizenship. Natural is good." Jason had brought me some clothes. We got me dressed. They put my left arm in a sling. It helped, but arranging the part that went over my shoulder was a little tricky. Once I had mastered it, we were out of the room. The hospital insisted I ride in a wheelchair to the exit. I think they hedge their bets. I think they want to be certain the patient they're releasing doesn't fall and break something on the way to the street. Whatever the reasoning, Jason delivered me safely into a waiting Uber, and we were on our way across town.

Fresh air smelled different from hospital air, of course. It smelled like freedom. There were a few bumps in the road that gave my shoulder a twinge, but I figured a way to cradle my left arm in my lap to minimize the shock. It was all good. As I watched the scenery change from the East Side to the West Side, I remembered our dinner the night before. It was so unlikely—my spending the evening with three men I loved and who probably loved me.

Jason was right, of course. He and George could well have been friends. Might still become friends, I decided, if the future had any mercy in it. I stopped worrying about sexual dynamics and historical intersections of hearts and bodies and started to feel intense gratitude for the wondrous people in my life. It was a good feeling. It was a necessary change of heart. A leap of faith, really.

When we got home, Jason sat me down on the side of the bed so he could remove my shoes and help me slip into the sandals I normally wore around the house. Other than that, we didn't get near the bed all day except to make love. Ah! Jason was a generous lover in ordinary times. That day, he took such care for my comfort and safety that my eyes welled up as soon as he slipped off my clothes and helped me sink into a great pile of pillows. "Don't move, Pauly," he said. "Just let me have my wicked way with you."

I did. I let Jason honor my body in his intuitive, careful, thorough way. He knew, of course, how much I craved his kiss. He gave me his kisses as freely as a modern mother gives her baby Cheerios. Only Jason's kisses were delicious and far more substantial. I accepted his attentions, his offerings. With my right arm newly unencumbered I was able to reach for Jason's face and caress him.

Jason carefully steered me in the direction of an explosion—not too soon, but not so late that my injured shoulder might tighten up. I tried to let my whole body go limp as I surrendered to the miracle of orgasm—that flood of sensation that is all about the self and yet—also—all about the beloved. When my breathing had normalized a bit, I said, "Jason, please come on my face. If you'll do that for me then I'll have sweet evidence that you really are here with me, that you really are home. Only then will I believe it."

Jason found a safe place to kneel, to my right, where he could deliver what I craved. I began to weep as he got close. And then Jason released a torrent of living fluid that washed over me and bathed my spirit just as surely as it bathed my body. We started to laugh. Jason kissed me. Big, cummy kisses. He tried to direct as much of the bounty as possible into my open mouth. It was true. Just as I had said. I was finally able to accept that Jason and I both were really home.

We lay quietly for a while. I had nearly dozed off when Jason said, "Paul, I don't expect you to stop loving George. I'm not stupid. I know it doesn't work that way. But if you've chosen me, I'll never question your heart." I drew Jason as close to me as I could. I knew, of course, that I didn't deserve him. And yet I found a new, steely resolve to get it right. To earn my happiness.

That afternoon, over a glass of wine, I said to Jason, "Darling, you can't keep neglecting your work like this. I'm fine. You need to look out for yourself."

"Pauly, I *am* looking after my career. I have a great network of colleagues. Part of what we love so much about our work is the flexibility. Clients don't pout when we send a sub. They understand that things happen in life. They're open to new people and new fitness ideas. And if they decide they prefer working with the sub, then they have my blessing. I'll get the next one. I know what I'm doing, Paul. Please don't fight me."

I surrendered, I suppose. It was an excellent first day home. Clyde and Lily were putting together a dinner to bring to our apartment as a welcome home. I was ready to see people and to eat and drink and feel normal. Maryanne phoned at 5:00 to say she needed to have dinner with a client. I wished her well and asked her to phone in the morning.

Clyde and Lily arrived with a huge array of tapas, some hot and some cold. We enjoyed Iberian ham, chorizos cooked and cured, *tortilla* (potato omelet), grilled eggplant in a spicy tomato sauce, plump shrimp in dense green olive oil with an overdose of garlic and a touch of chile, exquisite little heart-shaped roasted scarlet peppers stuffed with braised short ribs, olives, bread, Spanish cheeses. Lovely. Even though the treats all came from tote bags, it was quite different from previous dinners that week. We were home, first thing. I was able to wear real clothes and to sit in a real chair. And the only ex-lover in sight was the one who had forged bonds of friendship with me more than a decade before.

When our friends had left, Jason and I straightened up. Or rather, Jason straightened up and I supervised. As we got ready for bed, Jason asked, "How was your first day home, Pauly?"

"You were perfect," I said. "That's all that matters." It was a perfect day, really. And I was more than ready for a perfect—not drug-induced—night's sleep. And I got one.

There was no bounding out of bed in the morning—not for me, anyway. I remembered to move carefully to protect my still fragile shoulder. Jason was up before me, brewing coffee and simmering oatmeal. I slipped from the warmth of our bed to the warmth of the breakfast table. Lovely. Late summer morning sunlight streamed in from the living room windows while the air units beneath them purred along with their offering of coolness. Perfect.

"It's Thursday, isn't it?" I said. Jason smiled indulgently. It's remarkably easy to lose track of time when the routine is interrupted. "I'll call Jeremy this morning and see if there's anything going on at work that I should know about. I suppose I'm on sick leave."

"Of course you are, Pauly," Jason said. "You couldn't possibly go back to an office routine for another two weeks or so. Don't even think about it."

"You're right, of course," I said, "but the lawyer in me wants to know the terms." *The lawyer in me.* It was nearly a foreign concept that summer morning, and yet it had been at least half my life for nearly half my life. Hmmm. Definitely something to think about. "What are you up to today, darling?" I asked.

"I'm heading out in a few minutes," Jason said. "I have two clients, and then I'll be back in time to organize a bite of lunch for us. Is there anything you need from the outside world?"

"The only thing I need from the world is you, Jase," I said. And I meant it.

"I'm going to leave, Pauly," he said. "Drink plenty of water. And take your temperature this morning—but not after drinking hot coffee. The orderly told me how to seal up the wound with tape and Baggies so you can shower. We'll do that when I get back. Just call me if anything comes up."

"I'll be fine, Jason. Except for missing you. Sally forth, young man!" I demanded a kiss—a real kiss—and then he was off. I missed Jason terribly as soon as the door shut behind him. I wondered how I'd ever adjust to anything like a normal workday and normal daytime separations. I tried to stop thinking and start doing.

Chapter Fourteen

I phoned Jeremy right after Jason left the apartment that Thursday morning. I assured him I was recuperating nicely. "I was wondering, Mr. Cornell, are you up to signing a few papers?" he asked. I assured him I was. "Then what if I stop by your apartment this afternoon, at the end of the day, maybe about 5:00?"

"That sounds great, Jeremy," I said. "I'll look forward to seeing you then." I hadn't really thought it through, I suppose. Of course I wouldn't be able to discuss anything interesting with Jeremy while he was at his desk. Whether or not our phone conversations were actually monitored, there was no chance of my learning any office gossip while he was on duty. No. But a face-to-face would most likely yield the information I sought. 5:00. Perfect.

Next I phoned Clyde to thank him for bringing all the dinner goodies and for being my best friend. "Lily was such fun last night," I said. "No wonder we all adore her so."

"Yes, when her best self is on display," Clyde said. "The other one is not quite so pretty. But we don't judge our friends, do we?"

"No more than absolutely necessary," I said. "But then, you never judge anyone, Clyde, do you? You're such a good man."

"Shut up, Paul," he said. "Focus on healing, my dear. Let that beautiful mate of yours help you get well and strong, and maybe you'll work on your attitude at the same time." I assured him I would try.

Maryanne phoned a few minutes later. "Sorry I missed dinner last night," she said. "Lily told me you look terrific. And she's not one to sugarcoat anything."

"No, she's not," I said. "I guess it's official. I look terrific. When will I see you, Annie?"

"Well, it turned into a busy week. Will you save Saturday night for me?"

"Of course," I said. "I'm sure I can carve at least a few minutes from my mad social whirl."

"I'll call Jason this afternoon, and we'll plan something. I'd love to take you out, but I think it's maybe a bit too soon. I want to see you, Paul, and then I've got to head back to Buffalo on Sunday. And there's someone I want you to meet."

"Oh?"

"Yes, Pauly."

"Now who's being mysterious?" I asked.

Maryanne was too smart to take the bait. "Please let Jason pamper you, Big Brother. He's the best medicine there is. I'll see you on Saturday. I love you, Paul," she said. "Always did." And she ended the call. I was a bit puzzled. Not that I was so closely involved in Maryanne's life that I had any say in it. And yet ...? It was perplexing, but I still managed a nice little nap on the sofa.

My phone rang about 11:00. It was George. "How's our hero this morning?" he asked.

"Not very heroic, I'm afraid. Other than that, he's fine. How are you?"

"Terrific, thanks," George said. "I got used to seeing you every day for a while there. It seems strange to go back to the occasional conversation."

"Yes, it's all strange," I said. Whatever that meant. "It's nice to hear your voice."

"Yes. Paul, I had a thought: If you feel up to going out a week from Saturday, I'd like to have some people over for dinner. I won't be cooking—not to worry. Why don't you ask Jason what he thinks? I'm sure he has the best handle on your condition. Anyway, please think about it and let me know. I'd love to see you both."

"Thanks, George," I said. "That sounds lovely. I'll speak to Jason and give you an answer as soon as possible." I was less concerned about my shoulder than about the prospect of returning to George's apartment. With Jason! It seemed bizarre, and yet, why not? The ice was broken. There was no point in pretending that George and I had no relationship. We had history, of course. "I'll phone you Monday at the latest," I said. "Thanks again, George."

Jason arrived home shortly after George's call. And not a moment too soon, as far as I was concerned. How, indeed, would I settle into any sort of new normal without Jason at my side at all times? "I missed you," I said.

"I missed you, too, Pauly," he said. Jason looked at me indulgently. "I've brought you something special, dear." He produced a package that was not exactly gift wrapped, but it was *wrapped,* for sure. I began to undo the layers. The last one yielded to reveal a fancy thermometer, the kind you point at a forehead to get an instant, noncontact reading.

"Please, God, don't let me be normal!" I said dramatically. We laughed. *THE FANTASTICKS* was really before my time, not to mention Jason's. But I think many New Yorkers—the gay ones, certainly—remember the girl's plea for excitement in her young life. Because my mind works that way, I wondered how *THE FANTASTICKS* would play these days, considering that the fathers and the narrator cook up a scheme to stage a rape—in the sense of "to carry off."

Kidnappings of any sort, even for the most benign of reasons, are no longer stageworthy, I imagine. *The lawyer in me* says that, for sure. Maybe the show is not so sweet, after all. Hmmm. Nice songs, though. "Could we have a nap?" I asked.

"You can have anything you want, Pauly," Jason said. "Just let me organize things so we can have a bite." Jason unwrapped sandwiches that were stuffed with entirely too much grilled tuna and sliced avocado, and the whole-grain bread was smeared with pesto on one side and aïoli on the other. Yum. "What do you think?" Jason asked.

"I think I'll be big as a house if you keep pampering me this way. But I'm not going to worry about it. I have an excellent personal trainer."

"You bet you do," Jason said. "And your trainer says you should have a glass of chardonnay with your lunch. And you'd better follow orders." I did. Between greedy bites, I began to tell Jason about my morning phone calls. I told him that I thanked Clyde for dinner and that Jeremy offered to stop by with some papers for signing.

"He should be here around 5:00. I don't know how important the papers are, but I'm looking forward to hearing the latest from the office. Did Maryanne call you?"

"No, not since Tuesday. What's up?"

"She wants to have dinner on Saturday. Here, I guess. And there's someone she wants us to meet. Hmmm. I'm sure she'll call you today. Just keep it simple, darling," I said. "You know I'll eat anything. I only get picky when it comes to dick. That's why I chose yours."

"What a coincidence," Jason said. "My dick happens to be in need of attention. What do you think?"

"I think I'm the man for the job." We headed to the bedroom for a little afternoon delight. As before, Jason was very careful and gentle with me. Afterward, we took a short nap. And then Jason sealed my bandages with tape and plastic film so I could shower. Excellent! The afternoon turned into maintenance time. Jason removed my dressings, cleaned up around the wounds with alcohol swabs, dabbed on the healing ointment Dr. Shapiro recommended, and rebandaged. "I feel like a new man," I said.

"The old model was good enough, but I think I like the new one even better," Jason said. "Especially the new beard." He kissed me. I melted into a puddle of joy and uncomplicated love. "We have time to watch a movie before Jeremy gets here," Jason said. "What would you like to see?" I remembered a new series on Netflix that got a lot of hype for its gay themes. We settled on the sofa to binge-watch. It was entertaining—most of the time. I dozed off now and then. It was all good.

When the house phone rang, I became fully awake for the first time in hours. Jason asked the doorman to send Jeremy up. It was delightful to see him. We embraced—gingerly. "Have you ever been here?" I asked him.

"You had that holiday party, Pauly," Jason reminded me.

"Of course," I said. "What would you like to drink, Jeremy?"

"Gin and tonic?"

"Why not?" I said. Jason sprang into action and tended bar. Gin for Jeremy and wine for us. "Jeremy, I'm dying to hear what's happening at the Diocese. Was I the only casualty on Sunday?"

"No, there was a parish priest—someone from Westchester I don't know—who took a bullet in the hand. He's recovering, apparently. There were jokes about stigmata, of course. Diocesan humor is a little creepy, I always thought."

"Quite. What are they saying about me?" I asked.

"You know," Jeremy said. "On the surface, it's all compassion. But you're an attorney. If I were you, I'd look at my contract." I knew exactly what Jeremy was telling me, without having to draw it out or bore Jason with workplace tales.

"How many new hires in legal?" I asked.

"Only one, as far as I know."

"It'll take more than one man to replace me. Let me know when they get to three," I joked. "Thanks, Jeremy. I *will* look at my contract. Jason said I should be on sick leave for another two weeks or so before I can return to an office routine. I'll look into it. And Workers' Comp. I should know all about those things, but they never interested me before. Now they do."

"You look great, Paul," Jeremy said. "It's amazing what a few days of loving care can achieve. I'll confess I didn't see much hope on Sunday night. I prayed harder than I've prayed since I was twelve. And the way you look today is a perfect example of answered prayer."

"Thanks, Jer," I said. "If we're confessing, then I'll admit I wasn't so sure Sunday night myself. It could have gone either way. But every time I was ready to give up, I felt you holding my right hand and George holding my left hand, and I didn't want to let you two down. That was it, really. That and the fear of never seeing Jason again. That was what sustained me." It was the truth, of course. We were quiet for a bit.

"George said he told you about his dinner plan, for Saturday-a-week," Jeremy said. "I think it'll be fun, if you're up to it."

"Sorry, Jase," I said. "I didn't get to George's call. He wants us to come to dinner. He figured you'd know if it's wise for me to go out a week from Saturday. What do you think, Doc?"

"As long as there's no break dancing involved, I think you'll be able to handle an evening out by then. You can check with Dr. Shapiro when you see him on Wednesday, but it sounds doable to me. How did you leave it with George?"

"I told him I'd discuss it with you and get back to him by Monday. Should I accept?"

"Sure, if you want to. George will understand if you're not feeling up to it—closer to the date."

"Well, that's settled!" I said. "Jeremy, will you stay and have some takeout with us? What are we going to order in tonight, dear?"

"We haven't decided yet, dear," Jason said. "But I think it will taste all the better if Jeremy joins us."

"Thanks, gentlemen, but maybe another time?" Jeremy suggested. "I have a dinner plan. Which reminds me, I have to leave. Thanks for the drink, and thanks for looking so healthy, Paul! And thanks for taking such good care of him, Jason. Shit! I almost forgot! I need some signatures, Mr. Cornell." Jeremy pulled some papers from his bag, I provided some scribbles, and he put the papers back into his briefcase. There were embraces and semi-embraces all around, and then Jeremy left.

"Nice man," Jason said, as he straightened up and started to organize our evening.

"Yes," I agreed. "A remarkable man. I don't know what my desk would look like if Jeremy hadn't been assisting me the last two years. But never mind that. I don't even know what my desk looks like today. If indeed it still is my desk."

"That sounds a little morose, Pauly," Jason said. "I understand that you're uneasy about the future, but since when do you define yourself by your job?"

"Since never, Precious One!" I said. I invited Jason to come to me and let me kiss him. And as I did, I realized that I had placed my left arm around his perfect waist. Progress comes in tiny increments. And they must all be celebrated. We did. I felt wonderfully relaxed, except for a nagging question at the back of my brain—how did Jeremy know about George's dinner party?

Chapter Fifteen

Maryanne phoned Jason, of course, and they planned a pasta supper for Saturday evening. Jason wanted to make lasagne, and Maryanne offered to bring wine and some antipasto things. We decided on 7:00. Maryanne said she'd come early with her dinner contributions. I was looking forward to it, except for the "there's someone I want you to meet" part. That had me a little on edge. But why, really? Why should I second-guess Maryanne and her friendships?

Maryanne arrived six-ish with several bottles of red wine, some gorgeous Italian cold cuts, and the fixings for a big Mediterranean salad. And some biscotti to serve with coffee. She looked quite wonderful—beautiful, I'd say. Maryanne had always been beautiful, yet she had a new luster. I mostly watched while she and Jason organized our dinner. "I invited David for 7:00. He's usually very prompt." I shot Maryanne a look that said, "Information, please."

"His name is David Amsler," Maryanne said, "and he's an IT expert. We've known each other more than a year, but he's mostly in Tel Aviv and I'm mostly in Buffalo, so we haven't really had that much face time. This trip, though, our New York visits really overlapped. We've been seeing each other every possible moment. Clyde knows I haven't been sleeping in his guest room, of course, but I asked him to wait for an explanation. It's serious, Paul. I wanted you and Jason to be the first to know. I think you'll like David. He's a good man. And he loves me." Jason was the one who embraced Maryanne and expressed his support. I was the one who looked ready for more information.

"David is about your age, Paul. He and his wife married young, had two children, and watched their relationship fall apart. They haven't lived together in seven years, I think it is. She has her own life. David contributes to child support, of course. His daughter just started college, and his son starts next year. He may decide on Yale. David is paying the tuition. He and his wife have talked about divorce through the years, but it's a little complicated in Israel. Rabbinical Court and all. There was never a good reason to go there. Until now. They've both hired lawyers to work out a settlement. It should be over in two or three months."

I was a little cool when David arrived—on time, as predicted. I greeted him as warmly as I could manage—I do know how to host, after all—and I accepted the pretty flowers he brought. We had the perfect vase for them. Jason quickly arranged the flowers and put them on the dining table. So far, so good. I studied my baby sister's new beau. He was handsome, in a slightly rugged sort of way. Tall, fit, self-possessed, with a terrific smile.

"Paul," David said. "I'd have known you anywhere. It's uncanny how much you two look alike. Maryanne told me to expect that, but it's still a surprise. It's very kind of you to have me over, especially with your injury and all." He shook my hand again and smiled warmly. He turned to Jason and said, "And you, Jason, are just as I pictured you from Maryanne's description. Thanks for going to all this trouble."

"We're happy to have you here, David," Jason said. "Come, sit down and I'll get you a glass of wine. The Nebbiolo Maryanne brought is excellent." We sat. There were lots of smiles. David described— briefly—the project that brought him and Maryanne together and how pleased he was that it did. David was on his good behavior, of course, but he was as relaxed as any suitor could be at the first meeting with the family. I tried to be gracious. I'm sure I could have been easier on him.

It was a delicious dinner and a pleasant evening all around. David obviously adored Maryanne. Whether he looked into her eyes or touched her hand, there was no mistaking his warmth. I wanted that to be enough to satisfy me, but it wasn't, somehow. Under any other circumstances, I'd have found David delightful. But as things were ...?

After coffee, David said grateful good nights to Jason and me, embraced each of us, and headed back to his hotel. Maryanne turned to us for a reaction. Jason said, "Maryanne, I think he's perfect, and I couldn't be more thrilled for both of you." He embraced her joyously. Then Maryanne turned to me. My reaction was cooler, of course.

"He's charming, Annie. You love him, so how could he not be? But he lives in Israel, and he's married. If I've learned anything about love, it's that it has to be here and now and total. Lust is fun—until it isn't anymore. Don't make me say sexist things. I don't even think men—gay or straight—can settle for portions of a relationship. Not for long, anyway.

Women? Correct me if I'm wrong, but I think women are even more ill-suited to columns and cornices without a foundation. Sorry, darling. I don't mean to give advice, but I don't want to see you hurt."

Maryanne embraced me. Carefully. She said, "Pauly, thanks for being so thoughtful about this. There's more to it, really. David and I took an apartment yesterday, in Gramercy. I asked Lily to decorate it, but I didn't tell her it was for David and me. I just told her it was for a business associate. I'll come clean when everything is out in the open. We're going to spend as much time as possible there, together, and then head home when we have to. We'll be married as soon as we can. Here, I think. We want to make New York our home. Paul, please be happy for me."

"Look, Maryanne, I'd do the Stations of the Cross on my knees if I thought it would help you find happiness in your life. Just tell me what you want."

"I want your blessing, Paul."

"You've had my blessing since the day you were born," I said. "I thought a whole lot more about God when I was four than I do now. I figured if God sent you into the world, there had to be a powerful reason. And I've never had cause to change my mind. If David makes you happy, then go for it. And don't let anyone or any situation stand in your way." We were quiet for a while. Quiet and a little weepy.

I broke the silence. "Don't keep David waiting," I said. "Have a safe trip tomorrow—and phone me. Often!" Maryanne embraced me and held me for rather a long while. Then she kissed me goodbye and thanked Jason for the wonderful lasagne. A kiss for him and she was out the door.

I helped Jason with the cleanup. One-armed, but willing. Jason looked at me a little oddly, a little quizzically. I had never seen that look before. "What?" I asked.

Jason smiled and said, "I'm proud of you, Pauly. I was a little nervous about your reaction to David. I wondered if you were going to be negative about him. Maryanne seemed so happy, and you seemed ready to step on her happiness. Or so it appeared. I'm glad I was wrong. I'm glad you gave her the support she needed. And I think I love you even more because of it."

"I'll take your love any way I can get it," I said. "Jason, you're entirely too good. Could we leave the rest of this cleanup until morning? I want to hold you. I need to lie beside you in our bed and remind myself why I'm willing to get up in the morning." Jason put away the last of the lasagne—enough for supper for the two of us, luckily—and put the pan in the sink to soak. And then we went to bed.

I couldn't spoon Jason the way I wanted to. My shoulder didn't quite allow for that range of motion in my left arm. But we had worked out a hybrid spoon with me on my back and Jason carefully wrapped around my body. Close enough. His warmth penetrated all the way to my heart. "Thank you, Jase," I said.

"For what?"

"For loving me. Will you stay?"

"Hush, Paul," Jason said. "Of course I'll stay. For as long as you want me. Go to sleep, darling." I did as I was told.

We gave new meaning to Easy Like Sunday Morning. Jason and I shared coffee with hot milk and a piece of toast with good butter and orange marmalade. Perfect. We started on the Sunday *NEW YORK TIMES*. We were mostly silent, except for those occasions when I said, "Jason, I love you," for no particular reason. Perhaps I was attempting to make up for lost time. I had two years' worth of lost chances, after all.

"What would you like to do today, Pauly?" he asked.

"Other than staying as close to you as I possibly can?"

"Other than staying as close to me as you possibly can."

"What would the doctor say to a walk in the park," I asked, "if I wear a sling and we don't overdo it?"

"The doctor believes a walk in the park could have therapeutic benefits, as long as the patient stays very close to his caregiver." We completed our lazy morning and then slipped into the lightest clothing we owned. Central Park managed to enchant, even when the rest of nature had started to wear that burned-out late summer garb that makes us wonder what to make of a diminished thing.

"I think we should head home, Pauly," Jason said when we had walked for a while and savored the coolness in the shade of mature trees, as well as the energy of children frolicking in a sunlit meadow. "I don't want you to overdo it."

"No," I said. "I haven't admitted it, Jason, but this shoulder thing is a bitch. I've never been sick a day in my life. I don't know how to operate at less than full steam. You have to help me."

"Hush, Pauly," Jason said. "Let's get you home. I think you've earned a Campari and soda, or maybe a Negroni. What do you think?"

"You know what I think, Jason—what I've always thought: I think you're perfect. Let's go home." And that's what we did. Jason helped me out of my clothes and then changed my bandages. We relaxed and savored a long, cool libation. We settled on the sofa to watch a movie. The picture was boring, and I hadn't spoken to Clyde lately. So I phoned him.

"Maryanne said you'd fill me in," Clyde said.

"Yes, well, there's a fiancé, Clyde. Our little girl is not so little anymore. I'm sure you'll meet him next time. She wanted to tell Jason and me first. And there's never enough time, of course, when she's in town. But I think we'll be seeing more of her in the future."

"What's the verdict?" Clyde asked.

"He's great-looking, he's smart, he's gainfully employed, and he obviously adores Maryanne. So far, so good," I said.

"But?"

"But I'd feel a whole lot better about the whole thing if he didn't live in Israel and if his divorce were final. But don't ask me. Ask Jason. He's a whole lot more tolerant than I am. He puts up with me, doesn't he? Oh, and Clyde, don't tell Lily! It has to come from Maryanne. I'm sure she'll phone her right away to tell her the apartment Lily's finding a decorator for is the new love nest. But let them work it out."

"Of course, Brother dear," Clyde said. "I hope you feel as healthy as you sound. Which reminds me, are you going to George's for dinner on Saturday?"

"That's our plan," I said, "unless the doctor nixes it."

"Good," Clyde said. "Put Jason on. I want a medical report." I did as I was told. I returned to the dreary movie, which had started to pick up its pace. Even so, I couldn't help wondering why George invited Clyde to dinner. But then, why not? George, Jeremy, Clyde, Jason, and me. *Who else?* I wondered. It was none of my business, of course. I returned to the movie, which had slumped again, and I dozed off.

David called late in the afternoon, from the airport. Jason answered my phone, and they spoke first. And then Jason handed the phone to me. "Paul," David said, "I love your sister with all my heart. We want to build a life together, and we want you to be part of it. Maryanne adores you so. I get it. I didn't at first. I'm an only child. My parents thought of themselves more as pioneers than homemakers. Maryanne taught me about family. Will you be my brother?"

I said, "David, you don't need to say those things to me, but I'm glad you did. Maryanne is not only precious to me, but she has so much to offer the universe. I think you understand. I want you two to be happy, with all *my* heart. And yes, I'll be proud to be your brother." There wasn't much to say after that, except "safe trip" things and "yes, let's get together the next time you're in New York" and "yes, you mustn't miss your flight."

Jason looked at me. He overheard most of the conversation, of course. "Aren't you full of surprises, Pauly!" he said. "Will I know the man I'm going to bed with tonight?"

"Why wait until tonight?" I asked. We didn't wait.

Chapter Sixteen

The next week was mostly more of our new normal. Jason nursed me and worked a few jobs a day. We shared simple suppers and takeout. I even figured out how to grill a steak and assemble a salad with one arm. So I felt that I was pulling a fraction of my weight, anyway. I spoke to Jeremy most days, to keep my oar in at the Diocese. It looked as if I would indeed receive sick pay—for the previous week and the present one. After that? It was a question of how generous the Diocese wanted to be and how litigious *I* wanted to be. Future stuff.

I phoned George on Monday to accept his dinner offer for Saturday. "That's great, Paul," he said. "I'm delighted you feel up to it, and I'm looking forward to seeing you both. I hope you like Portuguese food. Have you met John Fonseca, the Bishop's chef? Of course you have. The Bishop will be out of town, and Jeremy persuaded John to come over and cook some traditional dishes. I think it should be great fun."

"Of course," I said. "John's a sweetheart. And cute, too."

"I haven't met him," George said, "but Jeremy assures me he's both competent and decorative."

"I wish I could say the same for myself," I said. "You'll fall in love with John. Or someone will, anyway. Thanks again, George. We're both looking forward to seeing you." I was pleased to be getting out of the house a little. But I was still nervous about returning to George's apartment—with Jason. And I was still wondering how Jeremy figured in all this. I didn't ask him. I didn't discuss personal matters with Jeremy at all on our business calls, of course. My questions would have to wait.

Jason took me to the hospital to meet with Dr. Shapiro on Wednesday, as scheduled. The doctor was satisfied with the surface healing and ordered the external sutures removed. He also tested—very gently—the extent of any mobility I had regained, which was little. "Don't be discouraged," he said. "I'm sure I warned you it will be a long, slow recovery. You're doing great, Mr. Cornell, thanks to your strength and to Mr. Novak's care. Carry on. Come back to see me in a week."

"Thanks, Doctor," I said. "Could I ask ...?" He stopped his exit and turned back to look at me. I said, hastily, "I've been invited to a dinner party on the weekend. I haven't really gone out so far, but it seems doable. What do you think?"

"That sounds reasonable, Mr. Cornell, as long as it's a quiet setting. Listen to your body. Good day to you both." And he was gone. Jason and I headed home and celebrated my good health with a careful romp in our bed. The next two days were unmemorable—except for the lovemaking. I've never forgotten a single embrace I've shared with Jason.

When we woke on Saturday, I felt strong and ready for an evening out. Jason had two morning clients to visit, and then he returned with a bottle of Port and a beautiful little plant—a sort of dwarf orchid with many blooms. "Let's work on that beard a little," Jason said. I was behind with grooming, of course. Jason snipped me into shape (tending to nostril hairs, while he was at it). I was starting to look human. "Very handsome," Jason said.

We allowed plenty of time for taping up my shoulder in advance of a shower. With the washing and grooming out of the way, it was time to attend to wardrobe. Jason helped me into slacks, a real shirt, and real shoes. How long had it been? I noted the feeling of confinement—especially from the shoes— but then I sensed the normality of being dressed, and that sensation outweighed any others. I was ready.

Jason slipped into his brand of evening wear: I had long marveled at how easily he could pull on slim black jeans and a soft, clingy top and look stunning. Cotton for summer, cashmere for cold weather. One stroke of a brush through his hair and he was ready for anything. Jason owned a suit, and I asked him to wear it once—to some Diocesan event at St. John the Divine. He looked great, of course. But Jason looked like someone else. Not like the man I loved. I never interfered with his wardrobe again.

Jason gathered up our host gifts and we headed out. The Uber driver offered a smoother ride than usual. Nice. I was feeling a little buzzy in my gut when we pressed George's bell and he buzzed us in. "I'm so glad you're here!" he called to us as we walked up to his door. "Let me get this hug right," George said as he embraced me from a safe angle. "You look terrific, Paul. I love the beard! I wouldn't have guessed it would be such a good look for you, but it is. Come in! Jason, how did you manage to grow even handsomer? Welcome!"

He ushered us in. George embraced Jason and kissed him—full on the lips. It gave me a twitch. Jason seemed fine with it. "Thank you both!" George said, referring to our gifts. "The Port will be perfect after dinner, and I have just the place for these orchids. How did you know?" He did have the perfect place for the little plant. He whisked off the wrapper and placed the pot on an end table by the sofa. It looked as if it was always meant to live there.

"Everyone's in the garden," George said. "You know everybody, Paul, but I think Jason needs to meet John."

"The garden?" I asked.

"Didn't I tell you? The owner of this building lives downstairs, and he loves to garden, but he doesn't have people over much these days, so he invited me to use it. I never have before, but this seemed like an appropriate occasion. Let me get you some drinks." We followed George to the kitchen, where he poured us glasses of rosé, and then we headed down the back stairs to greet the other guests. Gardens. Ah, gardens. *Urban* gardens. There's something so inviting about a leafy glade in the middle of Manhattan. Especially on a sweltering late summer day.

Jeremy greeted me first. "I talk to you nearly every day, and yet that doesn't seem to count. How are you? I love the beard. Very sexy!"

"I'm feeling great, actually," I said, "thanks to Jason and to you for managing what's left of my business life."

"Let's make this evening entirely secular," Jeremy suggested. "John wants to see you, and he's dying to meet Jason." I waved to John—with my good arm—as Jeremy steered Jason in his direction. Clyde embraced me.

"Paolino, if I didn't know you're an invalid," Clyde said, "I'd pin you against the garden wall and fuck your brains out. You look remarkably good. And young! I thought beards were supposed to be aging. Hmmm ... should I grow one, too?"

"Don't change a hair for me, Clyde," I said. "I prefer to love you just as you are." I looked at my old friend and let our history wash over me like a garden breeze. I wrapped my good arm around Clyde and said, "I don't think you know. How could you? I probably never told you."

"You're babbling, dear," he said.

"It's just that I could never have made it this far in my life without your friendship."

"Hush, Paul," Clyde said. "Why have you been keeping John from me? I thought everyone at the Diocese—other than Jeremy, of course—was exceptionally dreary. And now I learn you've been hiding a beauty from me. I'm sure the Bishop cares about John's cooking, but I'm much more interested in his eyes. Is John single, do you think?"

"I believe he is, actually," I said. "I think he's been so busy working since he moved to New York that he hasn't had time for anything else. I'm just guessing, of course. I'm also guessing that you could be the man to change his focus." Really, why had it never occurred to me to introduce John and Clyde? I felt like an idiot. And yet, things happen when they happen, of course.

George walked over, kissed me lightly, and said, "Isn't this a nice garden? I wasn't sure whether we should eat here or in the dining room. But I think the weather is going to be fine. Are you feeling up to having dinner outside?"

"Of course," I said. "Thank you, George, for including us."

"Paul, this dinner is in your honor, because you're a survivor." I was dumbstruck. No one had ever really spoken to me that way. George poured me another glass of wine. Clyde steered me to where John and Jason were talking.

John embraced me, carefully. He said, "Paul, I was heartbroken when I heard you had taken a slug. And so was the Bishop," he said with a twinkle. "But you look so healthy! I'm pleased to witness your recovery. I prayed for you, Paulinho," John said. "I visualized the chapel where Prince Henry the Navigator prayed for his sailors, and I prayed for your safety. And here you are!" George steered Clyde and Jason toward a table-setting errand, and John called out, "Don't take my sous-chef too far away. I'll need him soon."

And then John said to me, "I was afraid you'd never make that trip to Lisbon we talked about, Paul. Maybe you're afraid of losing Jason to some hot Portuguese guy. I don't think he'd be safe alone in Portugal, actually. But then I always thought *you* wouldn't be safe alone in Portugal. Perhaps if you two go together ...?"

"Only if you come with us," I said. "But really, John, I think you should go to Lisbon with Clyde."

"Interesting idea," he said. "Perhaps it occurred to me, just a few minutes ago."

"I'm delighted to hear it, John, but let me set some ground rules." I said. "Clyde is the best man I've ever known, and if you hurt him, I'll hunt you down and dismember all of your beautiful parts. Just so you know."

"Are you encouraging me to fall for Clyde, or … what?"

"Encouraging," I said. "Just do it right, please."

"I thought lawyers were supposed to be dispassionate."

"Yes, well, maybe I'm not much of a lawyer, but I hope I'm learning to be a good friend. What's for dinner?"

"Some traditional fare. A seafood combination to start—a sort of soup/stew. Very *Lisboeta*—and then *coelho em caçarola* just the way my grandmother made it. How's your Portuguese?"

"Nonexistent," I said.

"Good," John said. "Then you won't notice the bunny when he hops onto your plate. I'll make sure you get some of his liver—for healing. You don't look squeamish to me."

"I grew up gay in Buffalo. That's not for the squeamish."

"In that case, the rest of us will eat his heart. That's for courage. I don't think you need more. Paul, if you weren't already … overbooked, I'd make moves on you. But as things are? Where is that handsome husband of yours? He promised to help me in the kitchen. Jason has such beautiful hands. You probably never noticed them, Paul. I wouldn't trust just anyone to work beside me. I'm going to the kitchen. Send Jason if you see him. Dinner in about twenty minutes, I think." And he was off.

The weather did hold. It was a lovely evening—a little breezy, low humidity, for a change. We made our way to the table. Jason helped John bring our starter down the garden stairs and to the center of the table. When John lifted the lid, a great ocean current enveloped us. The pot contained a riot of sea creatures with mostly just white wine, garlic, olive oil, and a little saffron to marry them.

I think everything had a shell except for the monkfish. We started in. Everyone got a whole prawn from the surface display. Meaty tail, unctuous head. Lovely. Mussels, clams, crabs, fish. There were a few potatoes at the bottom of the pot that would have seemed incidental had they not been infused with the essence of the sea. We ate every bite and slurped every drop of the broth.

I was moved nearly to tears by the perfection of John's offering. It felt exceptionally good to be alive. I vowed to remember the sensation of wholeness. I looked at Jason, sitting across from me, and thought about how much I loved him. I looked at the others at George's table, and, of course, I loved every last one of them in various ways and for various reasons. John and Jason disappeared up the garden stairs to see to the main course. The rest of us—or rather the rest of them—cleared the first course things.

The main course—as John had revealed—was very grandmotherly indeed. Pieces of rabbit roasted with lots of olive oil and garlic, of course, and a hint of chopped tomatoes for moisture and sweetness. "I couldn't find an earthenware dish like this in cookware shops in Manhattan—not that there are any these days—or online, even," John said. "But there's a guy who works for me who grew up in Ironbound, in Newark. He was visiting his family last week, so he offered to shop for me. I hope my *avó* would be proud."

"I'm sure she'd find her *neto* just as charming as we do," Clyde said. Leave it to Clyde to be sufficiently multilingual for the occasion. The rabbit was delicious, and I ate some liver, as instructed. I always liked liver, actually. Who knows how tastes are formed? Salad, cheese, very good coffee, and then some little custard tarts. Perfect. George suggested that we have Port in the living room.

I made a pretense of helping Jeremy clear the table as the others headed indoors. I asked him, "Are you and George dating?"

"My, how quaint," Jeremy said.

"Cut the shit, Jeremy," I said. "You know I love you, and you know I love George. And if you two can find happiness together, then I'll be thrilled. You don't have to tell me anything. It's none of my business. But I'm hoping you can give George what I can't. He's waited a lot of years. He deserves some joy in his life. I'm just saying."

"Thank you for your blessing, St. Alex," Jeremy said. "I don't know for sure what George wants from me, but I could be ready. I could commit. It's been a while since I've entertained feelings like that. Not since I met *you*, really. That's all I know." I embraced Jeremy, and I felt foolish for having questioned him. And yet, how could I not?

"Jeremy, there's so much cleanup!" I said.

"Hush, Paul," Jeremy said. "Let's join the grown-ups." And we did. George's apartment was so inviting! It looked even more welcoming with people in it. Six men who liked each other—loved each other, for the most part. A perfect combination. I looked at George and decided he was satisfied with his hosting efforts, as well he should be. George looked so comfortable in his home—in his skin! As did Jeremy, of course.

I looked at Clyde as his arm fell casually around John's shoulders. I looked at John's contented response to their proximity. I looked at my glorious mate, and said, "Take me home, dear. The invalid needs his rest." We said our good nights and thank-yous. It was an ideal first outing for me, of course. I was full to bursting with good food, pleasure, and gratitude. "Thank you, darling," I said to Jason when we had settled into a taxi.

"For what?"

"For being you," I said. Jason snuggled up against my right side as we sped through a nighttime Central Park transverse and bounced our way home.

Chapter Seventeen

The days that followed George's dinner party were oddly peaceful. Jason and I settled into a routine in which he worked about half the day and then I helped with dinner and cleanup. As I became stronger and slightly more flexible, I went out for walks and looked for other forms of exercise. There were no push-ups in my immediate future, but there were other ways for me to stay active.

Jason began to conduct a daily afternoon therapy session—physical, that is. He was so gentle with me. John was quite wrong, of course, when he told me I didn't appreciate Jason's hands. I had admired them since the day we met. And never more so than when Jason applied his hands to my wounded shoulder. I'd never really analyzed it, but I suppose I believe in the curative power in the laying on of hands. It certainly worked for me.

Jason's hands on my body had always warmed me to my core. Our afternoon sessions were different, somehow. All right, I'm just going to say it—I felt healing energy emanate from Jason's hands and penetrate all the way to my bones. I felt progress with each treatment. And it was mostly just Jason's hands. He also knew how to manipulate the joints, of course. Tiny movements tested—and extended—my range of motion.

There were little milestones, like the first time I could scratch my ass with my left hand, and the day Jason removed my bandages and didn't replace them. Progress. It was all good, except that it told me I needed to think about my career, such as it was. I spoke to Jeremy nearly every weekday, while he was at the office. It wasn't enough. He started to phone me from home in the evening.

The next Sunday, Jeremy suggested, "Paul, I think you should come to the office. Soon. Tomorrow. There's only so much I can tell you about what's going on. You really have to see for yourself. They hide things from me because I'm just a clerical—and not a cleric." Just a clerical, indeed. Jeremy had been running my share of the office business for the last two years. And yet his position on the food chain was carefully set by his education and his job description. Was his race a factor? How often is race *not* a factor in the USA?

"Of course I'll come in tomorrow, Jeremy," I said. "But what about you? What about George?"

"Yes, well, there isn't much to report. I see George often. Sometimes I sleep over on weekends. He's kind, and honest, I think. I don't have to tell you how beautiful he is. We have a good time together. I want more. He doesn't seem to know what he wants." I made a mental note to see if I could maybe give George a little push. Gently, of course.

My first day back at the office seemed odd. Everything was very much just as I had left it three weeks before. And yet? Either *it* had changed or *I* had changed. Maybe both. Jeremy brought me coffee and a very slim file to read. "Most of your usual work is down the hall with Jeffers. Why don't you pay him a call this morning?" Jeremy suggested quietly. "If you want everyone to know you're back, he's your man."

I did exactly as Jeremy advised. I headed to the office just down the hall to put in an appearance. Jeffers was deferential. I went into my best hail-fellow-well-met routine. "You look terrific, Counselor," he said. "We were all so worried about you. And it's great to have you back. What sort of schedule do you have in mind, Paul? What do you feel up to?"

"I'm back to work, as of today, Will. Thanks for picking up the slack while I was away." I didn't mean the thanks, of course. I knew full well that Jeremy had done all the heavy lifting in my absence. But I played the game. The ball was in their court. The Bishop's court? I doubted he was much interested in personnel matters in the legal department. The less-divine members of the team would attend to such earthly things.

Jason had a delicious supper in the works when I got home. He helped me undress—though I could attend to most things myself. Tying and untying shoes was still a challenge. The therapy session that followed was the highlight of my day. Afterward we sat at the kitchen table and enjoyed a glass of wine. "So, how did it go?" Jason asked.

"Yes, well, I don't have a clear answer to that question, Jason. It was fine. It was creepy. It was familiar. It was different. It was welcoming. It was cold as a witch's tit. I think it's time we had 'the talk.'"

Jason looked at his hands and looked at me and said, "Since neither of us suddenly turned black, I'm not sure I know what 'the talk' is." I asked Jason for a kiss. He delivered.

"Do you really want to go all deep before dinner?" I asked. "This can wait." Jason went to the counter and finished assembling a plate of snacky things—salami, anchovies, roasted peppers, olives, aged ewe's milk cheese. He brought the plate to the kitchen table, along with some good bread and olive oil.

"So you don't have to think on an empty stomach," he said. He poured more wine. "Paul, talk to me. Please. You promised not to shut me out of your life again. Or at least I think you did."

"I couldn't shut you out of my life, Jason. You *are* my life," I said. "Look, I think we need to talk about finances and the future. I don't know how much longer my job will last. I don't know how much longer *I want* it to last. That's a lie. Jason, I want out. I want to take whatever severance they offer me—within reason—and move on. That job has paid the rent for five years, and I'm grateful for it.

"I practice gratitude for my job every day, Jason. But it's nothing like the gratitude I feel for you and our life together. I can't keep going to that office every day. It's beginning to suck the wind out of me. I'll find something else. Something better, I hope. Please forgive me, Jason, but I just can't do that anymore." Jason jumped up from the table and embraced me.

"If I had known how unhappy you were, I'd have urged you to move on ages ago," he said. "I hope I would have, anyway. Who knows? The important thing is that we can deal with this. We're not in danger of eviction or starvation. I can scale my income. It would mean longer hours, of course, but I can cover the rent, for instance. And you're nearly recovered. You don't need me so much anymore."

I grabbed Jason with all the strength in my good limb and said, "I need you more than I ever have, Jason. Please stay with me. Please let me share my life with you. Please let me hold you and feel you next to me in our bed. Please let me have the gift of your sweetness. Please let me look at you every morning and every night. Please let me tell you how much I love you." I was becoming a blubbery mess. Jason was patient with me, of course.

"Hush, Pauly," he said. "Let me work on dinner. Since we can still afford food, let's enjoy it." I wouldn't call it enjoyment, exactly—what I experienced that Monday evening. But there was a sense of relief, anyway. I had come clean about my feelings, about my hopes and dreams. Always therapeutic. And Jason made it clear that we were a team and that we could handle any situation that came along. I believed it—for the most part.

When Clyde phoned to invite us to dinner the next week, I was ready for something easy and fun. I knew the food would be good, since Clyde was a confident—and adventurous—cook. There was always some exotic cuisine he heard about from the books he edited or from his colleagues who edited cookbooks.

"Lily's coming. I don't get to see much of John evenings, but he'll stop by late—for coffee or a night-cap. So you'll get to see him. And maybe he'll sleep over. Paolino, I can't tell you how much I love having John in my bed. He's so gentle and kind. He almost reminds me of you—at his age, of course. It was sweet, wasn't it? What we had for a while there."

"It still is sweet, old man," I said. "What can we bring?"

"Just your perfect selves. I'll have everything else. I didn't realize it until this minute, but your birthday is only about six weeks away, so it's time to let Lily plan your party."

"Do I have to?" I asked. "Do I have to have a party?"

"Yes," Clyde said. "Next question."

"Will I have any say in it?"

"None. Lily will decide everything. And it will be the best party you've ever attended. So relax and enjoy it, dear."

"I have some news, dear," I said. There was no point in putting it off. "I'm leaving the Diocese."

Clyde paused for a moment and then said, "Good. Is there anything you need?"

"What do you mean?" I asked.

"Don't be coy, dear. Is there anything you need?"

"Oh, thanks, Clyde. We're fine. Jason's working, of course, and I'll get some sort of farewell gift, I assume. Let's not talk about it."

"Whatever you say. Just keep me posted. Lily and I each have a rainy-day stash, so you won't go hungry, and you won't go naked, unfortunately."

"This is not a grim situation, Clyde," I said. "It's a new beginning. I don't know what it looks like yet, but I know it'll be better."

"Of course, Paul. Do you want Lily to look around? She knows everyone, of course."

"Thanks, Clyde, but no. I'll figure it out. I won't ask Lily to job hunt for me. The birthday party is enough. Too much."

Clyde's house phone rang. "That would be John. May I phone you tomorrow?" Clyde asked. I was delighted, of course, that John and Clyde had found some common ground. It helped to soften the feeling of terror in my gut. Being unemployed was a concept I hadn't considered since I was a younger man. But, obviously, the time had come to consider it.

Chapter Eighteen

"Come in, beauties," Clyde said when we arrived for dinner. We brought him a bottle of good red from my "cellar" and a generous little box of saffron that had been a gift from one of Jason's more thoughtful clients. Lily greeted us warmly.

"You boys look terrific," she said. "Even the old boy."

"You have such a way with words, Lily," I said. "I love you, too"

"Speaking of old," she said, "I booked your party venue today, Paul. I won't tell you where. I want it to be a surprise. A very pleasant surprise. We'll probably have to blindfold you and then transport you to the party in some mystery conveyance."

"If you must, then have your wicked way with me, Lily," I said. "I learned years ago that it's pointless to resist when you've formed a notion."

"Never forget that!" Lily said. "I hope John understands, too."

I looked to Clyde for clarification. "Lily has an idea for John's future. And you know Lily's ideas. Let's talk about that after dinner." Clyde had prepared a Moroccan feast for us—a remarkable lamb tagine with prunes and olives and preserved lemon, which he served with couscous. The couscous was a little bland on its own but stellar with the sauce from the lamb. There was also a vegetable dish with chickpeas. Very satisfying.

Over fresh fruit and mint tea, Lily began to describe her plan for John. Clyde said, "Why not wait until John gets here? He should be along in thirty minutes or so. He needs to hear about this, too."

"You're quite right, Clyde dear," Lily said. Jason and I were intrigued, of course. But it looked as though we'd have to wait for John's arrival—which was prompt. It was a pleasure to see Clyde's greeting. He and John were so easy and comfortable with each other. Loving, I'd even venture to say. I decided John understood the quality of the man he was "dating." Quaint term. Clyde was obviously smitten. And they made an exceptionally cute couple.

By the time we had all greeted John and settled him at the table for some fruit and tea, Lily was bursting with her news. "John, the most wonderful career opportunity popped up today. I'm dying to tell you about it."

"But, Lily, I like my job," John said. "I'm not in the market for a new one."

"You will be when you hear this: I got you an interview with the Chesterly Group. I don't have to tell you they run some of New York's favorite restaurants, from trendy to traditional. And they're around the country and in the Islands, as well. They're assembling a team to visit their venues and rate them. Strictly internal stuff. Quality control. They already have a front-of-the-house person. Nice guy. I've known Raymond for years. You'll like him. Now they need a menu and presentation guy. So, the two of you go to lunch, mostly, plus the occasional dinner or event. And then you report to headquarters."

"But I'm not a restaurant critic, Lily."

"No, John, you're a chef. That's what they need. Hear me out." John was resigned. Who could argue with Lily, after all? "They need a team to look at all their restaurants with an outsider's eye. You'll be like professional shoppers, only you'll be professional eaters, too. You'll be a team, the two of you. Raymond can ask your opinion of the hospitality, and you can ask him how he liked the food. That will give your reports perfect balance. I think you should do it. The money's good. They want to see you in the morning. And then you're in."

"Just like that?" John asked. "Lily, do you really have that kind of clout?"

"Are you kidding? Half their customers are my clients. I'm a mover and shaker, Johnny. They owe me. I wouldn't send you there if it weren't a quality operation. It is. They'll treat you right, or they'll answer to me. And Hell hath no fury like a Lily scorned. And of course they know I wouldn't send them anyone but the perfect candidate. This is going to be good. Just do it, John. Take a job with sensible hours. Give Clyde the life he's missed out on—for the last decade. Do it for him, do it for you, and do it for me. I like to see my friends happy. Do it for Paul and Jason, for fuck's sake! They want to see Clyde happy as much as you and I do. And when you travel, Clyde can go with you. Hotel beds are fun once in a while." She was gilding the lily, of course (sorry about that).

Lily certainly had a way of turning the screws. And yet, she was spot on, as usual. John knew it. I could tell he did. John knew it was a career opportunity as well as a life opportunity. I imagined the pillow talk he and Clyde would share that night. It made me smile.

"What do you think?" I asked Jason when we had arrived home.

"About?"

"About how much I love you. About how happy Clyde and John seem together. About how infuriatingly right Lily can be. About my desperate need to make love to you."

"Hush, Pauly," Jason said. "Let's take one thing at a time. Let's start with the making love part." And that's what we did.

I had intended to phone Clyde in the morning, to thank him for a wonderful dinner, but he phoned me first. "We didn't get much sleep last night, because John had to dash home early to dress for his interview. I've never seen him in 'business attire.' But if he looks half as good in business attire as he looks in no attire at all, then.... Paul, have I ever told you about John's body?"

"No, dear, but I want to hear the news, first. *Then* you can tell me about John's body, and I'll be all ears."

"John phoned me a few minutes ago. He showed up, on time. The assistant welcomed him and offered him coffee. The partners arrived in fifteen minutes or so. They had a pleasant visit. They took John's résumé, for their files, but they only just glanced at it. They gave him an overview of the job and what they expected to gain from the feedback it produced. One of the partners said, 'Lily says you're the man we need, so that's good enough for us. Can we welcome you aboard?' John said, 'Yes,' and the rest will be history, some day."

"Clyde, that sounds perfect!" I said. "Is John delighted?"

"I think he is, Paul," Clyde said. "I *hope* he is. I want him as close to me as I can get him. But I also want John to do exactly what he wants. Lily pushed him a little hard last night, in case you didn't notice. I hope he doesn't resent it. I hope he doesn't resent *me*."

"Ask him, Clyde," I said. "You're the best communicator I know. Don't let this fester."

"No, I won't. I'll speak to him tonight. Now, I promised to tell you about John's body."

"Yes, you did."

"John has the most wonderful skin. I can't even describe the texture. 'Velvet' won't do it justice. Feeling John's skin is the most sensual experience of my life—after making love to you, dear. That goes without saying."

"Yes, well, you're changing the subject, dear. Let's get your story back on track."

"Quite. The only thing better than touching John's skin is tasting it. I've been taking a tour. Every region begs for a return visit. I can't select a favorite. But if I had to choose a position to stay in for the rest of my life, it would be with my face pressed between John's legs. He has the most extraordinary ass. I can't get enough of it. I don't think he's used to being worshiped that way. I think I surprised him. Pleasantly. I suppose I'll have to come up with more variety, but unless John stops me, I'll always head for the sweet spot."

"When are you going to start writing erotica, dear?" I asked. "You certainly have a flare for it."

"I can only go there when I'm in love. Which is how I intend to stay. Maybe I'll write a book this year, instead of just reading them."

"Please do," I said. "Your travelogue came to an abrupt end, Clyde. Is there more you want to share?"

"Let me roll John over and survey his front. Nice broad shoulders. Slim arms with steely muscles. Sensitive nipples—one nibble and I can get a rise out of him. A generous dick with even more generous foreskin, which is always fun to play with. I could spend hours with John's balls—and have. They're perfectly matched, but his left ball hangs slightly lower than the right. Keeps them safe, I read somewhere. Safety first, I always say. Paul, he's gorgeous, my skinny young Iberian beauty. If I can't keep him, it will break my heart."

"Now, now. Clyde," I said. "Of course you'll keep him. I'm the only fool on Earth who'd walk away from you. Other men know what they've got. Quality men. Like the one you found."

"Let's hope," Clyde said. "I didn't ask how you are, Paul. We were so focused on John's future last night that we mostly ignored yours."

"I'm fine, Clyde. Adopting a wait-and-see attitude, currently. That's code for 'I'm getting lots of sleep and ignoring the choices before me.'"

"You've earned that," Clyde said. "You should take all the time for healing that you need. Rushing into something new would be just as stupid as staying at the Diocese if it isn't right for you. How is Jason dealing with all of this?"

"He's so smart, Clyde," I said. "He makes me feel like an emotional retard sometimes. I thought I had learned a thing or two about life. But Jason just lives it. And he's willing to live it with me. And that's why

I understand so keenly ... your feelings for John. If Jason left me I'd go under."

"Shut up!" Clyde said. "No one is going anywhere. Except for you. You're going to take a long, hot shower, and then a short nap, and then you're going to phone Maryanne, because you don't speak to her often enough. And then you're going to eat some Greek yogurt and some cashews. And you're going to read something, for a change. And maybe then you'll be ready to welcome your Adonis when he comes home to you. Did I ever tell you what I really thought of Jason when you introduced us?"

"I remember you agreed he was handsome, and hot, and charming. And, of course, I wouldn't have fallen in love with Jason—totally—without your approval," I said. "You know that, don't you?"

"I took one look at Jason," Clyde said. "a long, easy-on-the-eyes look, and I knew he was right for you. I knew he could give you everything that was missing in our—historical—relationship. I fell in love with Jason, too, of course. Everyone does. But he wants *you*, Paul. Never forget that."

"Clyde, please don't give up on me," I said.

"Not a chance," Clyde said. "Take that shower."

Chapter Nineteen

"I know it isn't Thanksgiving," Jason said a week or so later. "And I'm not worried about money. But I know we can afford a ham and a turkey—today. And I think we should have a party."

"Really Jason, why do you want to have people over?"

"Because they're our friends. Because we love them. In different ways. Isn't that enough?" I couldn't argue with that. We set a date and started to invite people. Jeremy and George accepted. John was still working out his notice at the Diocese, but Clyde and Lily asked if they could stop by for a drink on their way to the theater. Jason's trainer buddies had other plans. We couldn't think of any other loved ones we wanted to include, since Maryanne was in Buffalo, and Jason's near-and-dear were not all that dear and in California, mostly.

Jeremy stopped by the evening before our party with the pecan pie he had promised to bake. He also brought sweet potatoes and collards and a box of saltines for the scalloped oysters. Jeremy stayed for a glass of wine and to help Jason with the prep. It was always a treat to see him. I didn't really want any news from the Diocese, but it was difficult to resist.

Bruce K Beck

"The Bishop has his knickers in a twist (as the Brits say) over finding a new chef. He even asked John to pass along recipes for some of his favorite dishes. I heard that John said 'no'. Good for him." That was enough for me. I suggested we talk about food instead. "I think you'll like the pie," Jeremy said. "It's not too sweet. What am I saying? It's mostly sugar, but it has an overdose of vanilla extract, which balances the flavor. Very New Orleans. But they know a thing or two in Alabama as well."

"Any state that produced you has to be worth saving," I said. "Thanks, Jeremy, for all your help. We're looking forward to seeing the two of you tomorrow." Jeremy kissed us goodbye and headed out. "Alone at last," I said to Jason. "I don't suppose you can spare a few minutes—or better still, a few hours—for your paramour." Jason surveyed the menu and the completed prep and decided he could put the kitchen to bed for the night. And then I took Jason to bed for the night. Lovely.

📖

I was helpful. In my way. I polished silver and buffed tabletops. I installed new candles. I even remembered to put a scented candle in the hall john. And I gave the carpets and the rest of the floors the once-over with the vacuum cleaner. The apartment looked great, and it smelled even better. Jason had gotten up at dawn to take the turkey out of its brine and to lubricate it and get it into the oven. It was official. We were throwing a party.

Lily and Clyde arrived first. They looked very glamorous, and they brought us a bottle of

Armagnac. "If that handsome mate of yours is responsible for the wonderful smells coming from the kitchen, then I think you should keep him," Clyde said. "And if he's responsible for how fit you look, then you'd better give him a raise."

"Jason, you've done wonders with him," Lily said. "No one would guess that he was at death's door just a few weeks ago."

""I love you too, Lily," I said. "Come in. We have a red and a white open. Which would you like?" Jason poured. I answered the door and greeted George and Jeremy. They also looked festive. It was that kind of evening. We realized that George and Lily had never met, so we remedied that situation. "George is at Temple Emanu-El," I said to Lily. "He knows everyone."

In no time at all, they were new best friends, as only New Yorkers can become. Lily gave George a handful of her business cards. Networking. I wondered if I'd ever learn how. It had been a while since our apartment had really welcomed guests. It felt good. It felt right. By the time Clyde and Lily excused themselves to head off to the theater, I was looking forward to our feast.

It *was* a thanksgiving celebration. It was about gratitude and friendship. It was about drawing a circle of safety around our little group. It was about love, of course. And it was delicious. Over coffee, Jeremy said, "I want a story. I want everyone to tell us something we don't know. Coming-out stories are always fun, except when they're boring. No danger of that, here. Speakers' choice. As long as it's honest." I was a bit trepidatious, but I agreed. Tequila helped. We put four numbers into a hat—a cashmere cap of Jason's, actually—and we drew. And then we adjourned to the living room. George drew #1:

"The truth is, I didn't grow up feeling all that different," George said. "Maybe I didn't grow up. But I had only slight realizations about my feelings for boys. Feelings for girls were socially acceptable, of course, and I had plenty of those. I dated a lot. I was Prom King my senior year in high school. I thought a lot about sex, like all boys. But I didn't think too much about my own sexuality until college.

"I was twenty—on the first day of a literature class—when I looked at the guy who was sitting to my right and thought, *Gott im Himmel! He's the most beautiful thing I've ever seen.* It was at that moment, right in the middle of class, that I knew my life would never be the same. I also knew I had to get close to that guy—to touch him, to embrace him, to kiss him. When he accepted my friendship, I felt truly alive for the first time in my life, really.

"I didn't know what to do with our relationship, other than to enjoy it. It had a fairytale sweetness to it, our time together. It was nearly a year. And then I was called home. And I realized, in the months that followed, that I lacked the courage to be the man my new friend deserved. So I ignored his letters and phone messages. And I might never have seen him again, except for chance.

"Paul, this tequila is delicious. Can I pour some for everyone?" George poured. Jason had drawn #2:

"I didn't like being at home," Jason said. "My grandfather was abusive, and my grandmother was drunk, most of the time. The hours I spent at school were the sane ones. I had some great teachers. I had always been a natural athlete. By my senior year in high school I trained my way into being a track star. It didn't have the same glamour and scholarship opportunities as the contact sports did. But I liked the discipline, and I liked being fit. There was a coach who took a special interest in my progress.

"The other gym teachers were kind of gruff. Sadistic, even. Most seemed to believe in the 'Lets see how long you can run before you throw up' school of coaching. I could take it. Many kids couldn't. But Mr. Gillespie was different. He seemed genuinely interested in our progress and our health. And I became his special project.

"Coach Gillespie and his wife didn't have any children. Once, when we were training for the All-State track meet, which we hosted that year, Coach said he thought of me as the son he never had. I was moved by it. I probably thought of him as the father I never had. I suppose I loved him. It was a new experience, so I wasn't certain. Even now I'm not sure what I felt for that man.

"It was a successful meet. I won all my events and even set a high school speed record for the 400m sprint. Afterward, we went to the locker room, as always, and Coach Gillespie took me to his office, where I lay down on his massage table, as usual. He started with my neck and shoulders—because we carry so much tension there. He worked his way down and gave extra focus to my legs, of course.

"When our massage session was over, Coach slapped me on the butt, and I got up and headed to the showers. It was all perfectly ordinary expect that I happened to glance at him, sitting at his desk, and notice that he was crying. Softly. I was eighteen. What did I know about the reasons a man might weep?

"I showered and dressed and headed to my grandparents' house. And I disappeared into my room to read and do homework, as usual. I didn't learn until I got to school the next morning that Coach Gillespie went home and blew his brains out with his hunting rifle. We were all in shock, of course. But I felt responsible. I felt that if I had done the right thing or said the right thing he wouldn't have killed himself. There was no one I could talk to about it.

"The funeral was a simple event. Suicide is usually frowned upon. It certainly was where I grew up. I couldn't look at Mrs. Gillespie. Surely she knew it was my fault. Surely she blamed me for her husband's death. I was still dealing with grief and guilt a decade later, when I met Paul. But he took me in his arms, and I knew instantly that I could shed the past and build a future with him. And I've never doubted my choice."

I had a special embrace and kiss for Jason, of course. Jeremy was #3:

"I always knew. I thought everyone did," Jeremy said. "But we didn't have gay people in Alabama, as far as I could tell. So I just masturbated a lot and prayed for forgiveness. Something changed, though, when I was sixteen. There was this nice young preacher who came to help our pastor that summer. He was recently ordained and looking for church experience. Lucky for me. Rev. Tobias was tall and slim and had beautiful hands and a great smile.

"One Saturday he asked me to show him my favorite fishing spot on the lazy little river just outside of town. I was happy to oblige. I was used to bringing home a string of crappies for our Saturday supper."

"Crappies? What are they?" I asked.

"They're little fish. Maybe they're some sort of bream. I don't know. They're tasty, and they're free. Mother didn't seem to mind cleaning them, and she was always grateful when I contributed to dinner. I loved my mother and wanted to be a good son. Rev. Tobias was gentle and fun to be with. And he was educated! That would have been enough for me to develop a huge crush on him.

"We set up our poles and baited our hooks. I showed Rev. Tobias my favorite techniques. We didn't talk much. Fishing is not a chatty pursuit. We started to catch fish. It was a good morning. When we had taken enough crappies for supper— Mother had already invited the Reverend to join us— we put our equipment away. But instead of heading back into town, Rev. Tobias wanted to stay and talk. There weren't that many men who wanted to talk to me, so I was happy to stay. We talked about life and God, mostly.

"When we rose to leave, Rev. Tobias said, 'It's such a hot day. Why don't we take a swim?' I was happy to comply. We took off our clothes and slipped into the slow-moving current of the river. Tobias and I swam and floated and splashed each other like kids. I had never had a Saturday afternoon friend quite like him. Maybe I had never really had a friend. It's possible. Eventually, we had to think about getting home. 'I don't want your mother to think I'm a bad influence,' he said. 'The sun will dry us, but it'll go faster if we wipe off the most of it.'

"He started from my head and worked his way down my body with his beautiful hands, whisking away any visible signs of river water. Before long he was kneeling in front of me as he finished rubbing my legs. He said, 'The Lord has blessed you richly, Brother Jeremy. Use your gift to His greater glory.' My 'gift' was standing at full attention, of course. Rev. Tobias took it in his mouth. I had never experienced such sensations.

"*His* gift was bigger than I thought possible. He took my hand and placed it on his dick, which then grew even larger. I was mesmerized. I sank to my knees and began to worship as if I had been doing it all my life. When Rev. Tobias was satisfied that I had served him properly, he lifted me by my shoulders, turned me around, bent me over, and put his beautiful hands around my waist. I widened my stance, instinctively, for stability. I thought I was ready for anything.

"When he entered me, the pain was so intense I had to stifle a scream. And yet, within minutes the pain began to morph into something quite different. Something ecstatic. Something like a burning love for God. Just before he came, he began to chant, 'Bless us, Jesus. Bless us, Jesus. Bless us, Jesus.' And then he filled me with the Holy Spirit, as well as his holy water.

"When the sacrament had ended—and it was more intense than anything I had ever experienced in church—we stood, dressed, and gathered our things. Just before we left the riverbank, Rev. Tobias kissed me lightly, put his hand on my chin, and said, 'You're a good man, Brother Jeremy. God has great plans for you.' And then we headed back to town— me to give my mother the fish we caught and Rev. Tobias to change for dinner. He showed up on time and was a genial guest. Country preachers all know how to earn their supper. I loved being with him, even across the dinner table. Every one of his smiles seemed just for me.

"Rev. Tobias was in town for another month or so. The church had found a tiny apartment for him above the hardware store. He asked me to stop by a few times to help with something or other. It was summer, so my time was unstructured. I could disappear for hours and no one would notice. The time we spent in his apartment was quite different from the time we spent at the fishing hole. We lay down on his bed. Rev. Tobias made love to me. Adult stuff. I felt like a tourist in a new land.

"Tobias was only, what, six years older than I was? I think most of it he made up as he went along. I know I manufactured my responses on the spot. It was lovely. I just thought of a great title for my autobiography: *EVERYTHING I KNOW ABOUT SEX I LEARNED AT SIXTEEN*. It's true, really. I was lucky to have a gentle teacher. And I'll always be grateful to him."

"I want you to write that book, Jeremy," George said. "I'm going to start a crowdfunding page in the morning."

"I'll help you," Jason said. "The world needs that book, Jeremy. Paul, it's your turn. Tell us something we don't know, oh, Mystery Man." I didn't want to. I only spoke because the others had done it, and because I had promised Jason honesty:

"My father used to beat me. On various pretexts. It was a standard part of my childhood. I have a small scar beside my right eye and a large scar on my back. That's the one I always said came from falling onto a broken tree limb out in the woods. I'm sure there are others. I stopped counting them a long time ago.

"The beatings were unremarkable until the day—when I was maybe fifteen—when Dad walked into my bedroom—without knocking, of course—and caught me beating off to a magazine full of naked men. He dashed to my closet and demanded to know, 'Where are your golf clubs?' I refused to tell him that I had just stashed them in the basement the day before.

"That left him my tennis racket, which he quickly broke over my back. And then it was mostly his fists. Dad punched me. Repeatedly. I took it. I remained standing while he slugged me over and over again until his hands were too bruised for him to continue. Mother and Maryanne were in the hall just outside my bedroom door. Mother had never been able to protect me from Dad's attacks. I suppose she tried to protect Maryanne. But I couldn't swear to it.

"Maryanne ran into the room and threw her arms around me. I quickly put her behind me, on my bed. I stood between my father and my little sister. Like a fucking oak tree. I absorbed Dad's rage. If he had turned it on Mother, I'm not sure exactly what I'd have done. Maybe I'd have let him beat the shit out of her. I don't know. But if he had so much as touched Maryanne, I'd have ripped him apart. I think he knew that. I think we came to an understanding that day. And he never laid a finger on me again."

Jason put his arms around me. We were silent for a while. "My, what a festive story!" I said. "Can I get anyone another drink?"

"*Everyone* will have another drink," George said. "Did you think you could clear the room so easily?" George walked over to me and kissed me on the forehead. He put his hand on my cheek and said, "My little *Sonnenschein* has more clouds in his past than

I could have guessed. It's no wonder that he's so radiant now." Jeremy walked over, sat on the floor, and put his head in my lap.

I was enveloped—quite literally—by extraordinary men. I let them comfort me for as long as I dared. And then I stirred and said, "I could get used to this arrangement of beautiful bodies—all of which I know well, of course—but I don't think it's practical. I think we should divvy up the leftovers and see if we can kill the last of the tequila." We disentangled ourselves.

Jeremy and Jason attended to practical matters. They were deciding on Ziplocks and Tupperware and totes. They were intent on the future nourishment of our families. I asked George to come to the bedroom to look at a few rare books—religious tomes, of course—I had acquired when a strange antiquarian bookseller went out of business the year after George left Columbia.

"George, I know it's none of my business ..." I started.

"And you didn't even have a Jewish mother," George said.

"That's fair. George, I want to tell you how much I love you and how much I love Jeremy and how much I love the two of you together. And here's the part that's *totally* none of my business—I want to know why Jeremy hasn't moved into your home and into your life, really. And into your heart, I think. I don't get it."

"I think you do, Paul. I think you get it. I think you understand everything about my heart, considering that it's been yours for the last twenty years."

"Help me, Jesus!" I said. "Don't lay that on me, George." I tried to back off from a confrontation. I considered closing the bedroom door—to contain the storm. But I couldn't do that to Jason. It was his home, too. I did stick my head out the bedroom door to say, "Don't mind us. Unfinished business."

"George, when you disappeared nineteen years ago, you forfeited all rights to the moral high ground. You talk about your feelings as if they were independent of mine. You put me through hell, George. You spoiled me for other men. Clyde and I might still be lovers for all I know, if you hadn't been in bed with us. And you nearly wrecked my life with Jason. Forgive me if I've decided to put my needs above yours."

When I had cooled down, I dared to look into George's eyes. I saw such wells of sorrow that I said, "George, don't do this to yourself. Don't do this to the memory of what we had. Jeremy loves you. Let him into your heart. He'll give you a reason to live. He'll give you so much more than I ever could. No, George. No. I can't be what you remember. Release me."

"Is that really what I've been doing?" George asked. "I suppose I believed that if I kept the flame burning—if I maintained the purity of my love for you—that it might almost be like holding you in my arms, Paul. When I did hold you again, I hoped, against all odds, that we could put the past aside and create a bright new future together. But I left out the part about earning my way. *I* should know better— a business major."

"You've earned a right to happiness, George," I said. "Please tell me you'll embrace it."

"I will, actually," George said.

"How many more turkey dinners do you suppose we'll have to eat?" I asked.

"I'm looking forward to every one of them," George said. "Do you really think Jeremy will have me?"

"I know it," I said. "Take him home, George. Let him love you. You'll never regret it." George and I headed for the kitchen, where Jeremy and Jason had organized all the remains of our feast. The four of us polished off the tequila—a very smooth *reposado*—and then it was time to call it an evening. Jason and I embraced our guests, individually and collectively, and they headed for the door.

"Don't forget the birthday party," I said as they were leaving. "You'll hear from Lily, of course." Jeremy gave me a last kiss, and they were off. I turned to Jason and said, "Wow, what a lot of work for you!"

"Hush, Paul," he said. "I told you I wanted to do it. Thank you."

"For?"

"For your honesty."

"Yes, well, I have my moments," I said. "Will you allow me a few secrets in the future?"

"Not a one," Jason said. "Let's turn in." As we were brushing our teeth, Jason gave me his new quizzical look. "What were you and George talking about?" he asked.

"Besides how much I love you?"

"Besides how much you love me."

"We were talking about the past. And about how much more wonderful the present is. Will you come to bed, please? I can't sleep without you beside me, Jason. And I've spent too many mornings without you in my arms. Come to bed. Please." And he did.

<u>*Chapter Twenty*</u>

"Tell me, Doctor, am I well enough to attend a birthday party tonight?" I asked Jason.

"Turn your head and cough," he said. "And I should probably perform a prostate exam before I release you."

"Yes, please."

Jason kissed me. His kisses had warmed my heart since our first. I wondered why I had ever held him at arm's length—why I had ever been less than all in. Blame it on my youth. "I'd say you're well enough to run a marathon," Jason said. "Let's take it easy, though. Lily won't be pleased if you show up looking all hot and sweaty."

"Then you'd better stay home, Jason, because I'm always hot and sweaty when you're around me," I said.

"Age hasn't mellowed you," he said. "Good. I've always been happy with the Paul I fell in love with. Will you arrange to keep him around?"

"I'll do my best. What should I wear tonight, Jason? Where are we going?"

"I have the address, but I forgot the name of it," Jason said. "I know it's an event space on a high floor. You know Lily. It will be very glamorous. Why don't you wear your black velvet jacket? It's just turned cool enough for that. No tie, I think. Maybe a silk shirt?”

“What about pants?” I asked.

“I always liked you best without them,” Jason said, “but maybe tight jeans. No underwear. Definitely.”

“Yes, Doctor,” I said. “Do we have time for that examination before we have to dress?”

“There’s always time for that.” We went to bed. All I ever really wanted—all I ever really *needed*—was Jason’s skin against mine. Jason in my arms. Jason beside me. But he was intent on giving me a special birthday blowjob. How could I refuse? I’d have preferred more kisses, but I accepted his expert oral tribute. And then I demanded that he surrender his exquisite body to my own considerable oral skills. Happy birthday to me!

Autumn in New York! The changing of the seasons is stirring in all temperate climes, I suppose. But I lived in New York—by chance and by choice— and nothing other than sleeping with Jason was more bracing than experiencing the first cool days in the City. When I was a child my October birthday meant that the first snows of the season might already have blanketed Buffalo. But when I became a City boy, I learned to expect a certain crispness in the air and a golden glint to the afternoon sunlight that exist in no other season.

As much as I hated fuss, I resigned myself to the prospect of Lily’s party. I knew she wanted to honor my milestone, and I knew she’s do it well. And I knew we would drink exceptionally well, thanks to Lily's skill at getting donations from upscale booze brands. Her clients drove the New York City business for those companies, after all. They were happy for Lily to include them in an entertainment she designed. And I was happy to accept. But otherwise, no gifts! That was my ground rule. Lily promised to abide by it.

Jason was right, of course: It was a very elegant space—high ceilings, soft carpets, dramatic lighting, with a bar in the center of the main room manned by two exceptionally cute bartenders. But then, aren't they all? I wasn't certain about the guest list, other than my loved ones and a few of Jason's friends. I hoped that Maryanne could make it, but Lily was tight-lipped about the particulars.

I assumed Lily would sprinkle in a few of her clients who liked a good party—for atmosphere and for networking. I had told Lily, firmly, that I would not welcome her help with job hunting. But who knew? I might just start my forty-first year with a new position. Stranger things had happened at birthday parties, after all. I tried to remain open to serendipity. Clyde and John owned the first familiar faces I spied. Good.

"Congratulations, old man," Clyde said as he embraced me.

"I'll remember that in January when we celebrate yours," I said. "John, you're very brave. And very handsome, I must say. Corporate life obviously agrees with you. Or does it have something to do with my best friend here?"

"It has everything to do with Clyde," John said.

"Good answer," Clyde and I replied in unison.

"Whatever you two are doing, keep doing it," I said. "I've never seen either of you so radiant. If I didn't love Jason so totally, I'd be jealous." Jason smiled indulgently. On another occasion he might have reined me in a bit. But under the circumstances.... "Thanks for coming, both of you," I said. "It wouldn't be a party without you."

And then came the first unexpected event of the evening. "Dr. Shapiro! What a nice surprise," I said. "Thank you for coming." I shot Jason a look, of course.

"When Mr. Novak told me about your celebration, I wanted to stop by to make sure you're behaving yourself," the doctor said. "I had a hand in putting you back together, after all."

"It was more than that, and I hope you know how grateful I am," I said. I embraced him. It seemed odd, but he seemed comfortable with it.

"Please meet my wife, Miriam. Dear, this is Paul Cornell and Jason Novak." I was quite shocked, actually, to see the doctor—in civvies—and his handsome wife. We made our greetings. "We can't stay," he said. "We have another obligation. But maybe a glass of champagne before we go?"

Jason quickly rounded up some bubbly and some little smoked salmon things as well. We drank, we talked, we munched. I detected Leo Sager singing "More Than I Can Say" under our conversation. And then the doctor and his wife wished us a good night and headed on to their next event. "I'm not very good at handling surprises, darling," I said to Jason. "Promise me there won't be any more tonight."

"I never make promises I can't keep," Jason said. It was true, of course. Lily greeted us. She looked stunning in a swath of sheer silk that seemed to defy gravity as it clung to her bosom and avoided her back. Perhaps I hadn't known what a beautiful back she had. Perhaps I had underappreciated Lily for the past decade. Perhaps I might actually learn something on the occasion of my fortieth birthday. Stranger things had happened.

"You look good enough to eat," Lily said to me.

"Ditto," I said. "Why have you been hiding that body of yours?"

"I only share it with a select few. Jason knows the entire landscape," she said as she hugged him. "We're going to have a good crowd tonight. Happy birthday, my dear." I embraced Lily as warmly as I dared, considering the seeming fragility of her gown. It was the creation of one of her designer friends, no doubt. Lily was not one to risk a wardrobe malfunction. Her dress was probably as strong as armor. What did I know?

Jason steered me toward the entrance, where George and Jeremy were arriving. "I'm so glad you're here," I said to George as I greeted him. "It's good to have an older man in the house." George had turned forty in the past month. "Do you have any advice for me?" I asked.

"I do, actually," George said. "I can advise you—based on my longer experience of life—to resist advice from old codgers. Paul, you've learned so much more than I have," he said as he embraced me. "And you wear it well. Keep Jason close to you always. And I hope you'll keep Jeremy and me close, too." I got a little weepy for the first time that evening.

"You're a gift, George," I said. That was all I could manage. He was so handsome, and so warm and loving. I think I realized—just at that moment—that I could actually keep him. That I had been exceptionally foolish to worry about choosing between George and Jason. That my heart could expand beyond my previous estimation to include all the most important people in my life. Without equivocation. Without apology.

Jeremy greeted me with a birthday kiss. "You look like an answered prayer," he said. "Happy, happy!"

"And you look like a little bit of heaven, but then you always do. Welcome to whatever Lily cooked up. I haven't seen much of the food yet, but the bar is full of promise. Fire and ice, I'd call it. Don't miss the chance to get a smile from the brunette. I think he gives one with each drink. Jeremy, it's so good to have you here. I don't have to tell you how pleased I am to see you and George together."

"Let's talk later," he said. "

I'd have been perfectly happy on a champagne diet, except that the food was so tempting. I found myself constantly drawn to the mountain of raw oysters that seemed to replenish itself as if by magic. And hot young guys and gals quietly circulated through the room carrying trays of small savory creations that looked every bit as delicious as they tasted.

I didn't realize until about an hour into the party that the background music was a carefully curated playlist of 1980 hits. I wondered if *I* had matured as gracefully as they had. Diana Ross was singing "I'm Coming Out" when Maryanne and David arrived. I was delighted to see them—both. "Did you ever think we'd be where we are today?" I asked her.

"Yes, as a matter of fact," Maryanne said. "I always thought you'd grow up to be handsome and accomplished and that I'd fall in love with a wonderful man. Happy birthday, darling." It *was* a happy birthday, of course. With Maryanne's arrival, it felt complete. David embraced me warmly.

"We have a gift for you," David said.

"No gifts, please," I said.

"Actually, it's a gift for *us*. Let me get Maryanne a glass of champagne, and then I'll tell you all about it." I hadn't known that David had a flair for mystery. I looked at Maryanne, and she gave me her best "Let David do it his way" look. He returned with a waiter carrying a tray of drinks. "Where's Jason?" he asked.

"He's just over there," I said, "talking to some colleagues of his. I'll get him." I walked over to tell Jason of Maryanne and David's arrival. He quickly excused himself, and the two of us headed toward my sister and her beau. Jason greeted them warmly, of course. I loved that Jason was so easy with his affection for the important people in my life. Mostly, of course, I loved Jason. The Manhattans were singing "Shining Star" in the background. Indeed.

"Maryanne and I have an announcement to make," David said after the greetings and after he determined we each had a glass of bubbly. I assumed David's divorce was final and they had set a wedding date. "We formed a corporation yesterday," David said. "Maryanne and I are now partners in a new IT firm called Communication, Inc. We already have a number of clients we can bring over from our current work, and the rest of the client base we need we'll find as we go along. What do you think?" he asked Jason and me.

"It isn't the partnership I was expecting, but it sounds terrific to me," I said. "Congratulations to you both!" We drank a toast to the new venture, and there were hugs all around.

"There's more," David said. I told you he had a flair for suspense. "We need a corporate attorney, Paul, and after careful deliberation, we've determined that you are the man for the job. What do you say?" I looked to Maryanne for confirmation. She was beaming.

"Yes, actually," I said. "Yes, I'd be honored to work with you both." Weepy #2. Was I shocked that my career had suddenly taken a new turn? Not in the least. I always expected change and progress. Didn't I? Kool & the Gang crooned "Celebration." Yes, indeed. Jason squeezed me with welcome force. "Are you happy, darling?" I asked him.

"If you are," he said. "It sounds perfect to me, but I'm not the one who has to show up at the office every day. Talk to me, Paul."

"With the greatest pleasure," I said. "I'm a good lawyer, and it's time I flexed my muscles again. Working with Maryanne and David is the best situation I can imagine—besides living with you, of course." Jason congratulated David again, and I said to Maryanne, "We haven't talked lately about your love life, Annie. The two of you seem so easy together."

"I couldn't be happier, Pauly," she said. "Having you with us makes it perfect. We looked at office space this morning. It's almost a done deal. One of the new high-rises in midtown. It seems entirely too tall to be safe, and yet the views are breathtaking. You can choose whatever office you like." Maryanne kissed me.

"What about Buffalo?" I asked.

"Yes, well, I've been wrapping up my work there. I'm keeping my apartment—for now, anyway. The rent is a bargain, by Manhattan standards. We'll need someplace to stay when we visit—about once a month, I'm planning."

"What does David think of Buffalo?" I asked.

"Pretty much what you and I do, I think. I took him to meet the folks."

"Shit!" I said. "How did that go?"

"As you'd expect. David was charming. They were reticent. Mother asked him if he was Jewish. And then things got really icy. We didn't stay long. But then I never do these days. Anyway, I introduced them to my fiancé, and that's that. I'm not inviting them to the wedding."

"Which will be?"

"We're thinking maybe in the spring. There's so much happening, Pauly. We want to get the business up and running first. We'll focus on the personal later. Meanwhile, David's so easy to live with. He's kind and generous and protective. In fact, he reminds me of you sometimes." Weepy #3. "I'm so glad I'll be seeing more of you. And Jason, too, I hope. I'll text you in a few days and we'll get together to talk about the business. Happy birthday, darling!"

I looked at Jason and David talking and laughing together, and I realized how glad I was that Maryanne and I had each managed to fall in love with a good man. And speaking of good men, Jeremy signaled to me from across the room. I left my sister in the company of her mate and mine and went to join Jeremy.

"I wanted to wish you a happy birthday," Jeremy said, "and I also wanted to thank you, Paul."

"For?"

"For teaching me about love."

"I'm not following you, Jeremy. All I remember showing you was a man who can't keep it in his pants."

"That's *your* version of reality," Jeremy said. "I saw someone quite different, Paul. I saw a man who's a slave to love, really. A man who is capable of anything in the service of love. I asked you to come to my bed, and you did it with *love*. And you changed my life, Paul. Rev. Tobias taught me about sex. *You* taught me about love."

"Fuck!" I said.

"I'd love to, but George and I decided to try monogamy. What do you think?" The Pointer Sisters sang "He's so Shy."

"I think you're among the world's great beauties, the two of you. And I like you and George together. Very much. You waited for him, Jeremy. You let him figure out his heart. I respect that."

"I know you had a hand in it, Paul," he said. "George told me. He said you convinced him to release the past and embrace the present. He needed that push. And you're the only man who could have given it." Weepy #4. It was that kind of evening. I embraced Jeremy and walked him to where George was exploring a platter of *pâté de foie gras—truffé*, of course. We shared a group hug. I savored the individual and highly complementary scents of two lovely creatures. Life was good.

Lily turned down the music right in the middle of a Stevie Wonder song. She took a microphone and said, "Thank you all for coming tonight. I couldn't let Paul's passage into middle age go uncelebrated. I've known him for a decade now. I've watched Paul do a few foolish things—who doesn't?—but I've never known him to be less than a devoted friend and a kind and caring man. He's smart. He's hot. And he has excellent taste in men. I'd trust Paul with my life, actually. There was a time not long ago when I wasn't so certain about that. But Paul redeemed himself. I guess that's what can happen when you hang out in churches. I believe it has more to do with the love of a good man. And in that department, Paul is richly blessed.

"I met Paul's best friend, Clyde Hutchings, first. At a literary event. There were still real publishing houses a decade ago. Hard to believe, isn't it? Clyde and I fell in love—I'll speak for myself. Paul was part of the package. 'Love me, love my dog.' And I did. And I've only regretted it just the one time. But never mind that. Mostly, I've been pleased and proud to call him my friend. And I've watched with pleasure the joy he brings into other lives. So, on the occasion of his new-found maturity, I give you Paul Cornell!"

I was well oiled—but in a good way. I had to take the mic Lily offered me. I said, "Thank you, Lily, for this sumptuous party, and thanks to all of you for being here to share it. I know I don't deserve it, but I'll take it anyway. All that I love most in life is in this room tonight, so I feel truly blessed. I didn't know what to expect from turning forty. I have a tendency to ask my friends and loved ones not to give up on me. And you haven't. I'm humbled by it. I couldn't have dreamed up all the kindnesses I've experienced just tonight. And so I'm going to return the mic to Lily before I make an even bigger fool of myself." Polite applause.

Jason embraced me and led me out of the spotlight. With Stephanie Mills singing "Never Knew Love Like This" in the background, he said, "Paul, I think we should get married."

"Why?" I asked. "Why would you want to marry me?"

"Because I love you, and because you're such a good man." Weepy #5.

"Jason, you were so patient with me even when I was acting like a great big jerk. And I'll always cherish that. Of course I'll marry you. Even *I* am not jerk enough to turn down an offer like that. Name the day. I'm in for the long term, darling. But it will change us, you know. Marriage."

"How so?" he asked.

"Boyfriends and husbands are different animals, or so I'm told. I want to be a husband to you, Jason. If it's what you really want. There's no one else I can imagine spending my life with." Jason enveloped me in the warmth of his embrace. His strength made me feel safe. And his love made me feel whole. "I don't have to ask you to be gentle with my heart. You've been just that since the day we met," I said. "Should we announce our engagement?"

"We'll have to tell some people. Soon. Most of them are in this room. There's no time like the present, Paul."

"But really, Jase," I said, "does it have to be a Wedding by Lily? Couldn't we just elope?"

"I doubt it," he said. "But let's take one thing at a time. I'll get the microphone from Lily. Who goes first?"

"It was your brilliant idea," I said. "You should make the announcement." He went to find Lily and to locate the mic. We headed to the most central and visible part of the room for the second time that night. Lily called for attention. And when Lily spoke, people listened! A hush fell over the room. She handed the mic to Jason.

"All the people that Paul and I love best are gathered in this room tonight," he said. "So we wanted you to know that a few minutes ago Paul agreed to make me the happiest of men. We're going to get married." The room erupted in applause and joyous shouts. And then I had to speak. Jason was a tough act to follow.

"Jason has blessed my life since the day he walked into it. I never dared to think that I could be so completely happy, and yet I am. So when he popped the question—not on one knee, I just realized [polite titters]—I didn't hesitate to say yes. Of course we want all of you present on the big day—whenever it is. Lily, please, something simple," I said.

"Not on your life," she said. She took the mic and said, "I'm so glad you're all here this evening. The night is young!" Lily embraced Jason first, of course. But her embrace for me was nearly as warm. "Christmastime, I think," she said to both of us. "Very festive. And I have a friend at Cunard. The middle Caribbean is lovely that time of year. Just right for a honeymoon."

"We'll talk," I said. "Lily, this is amazing, what you've done for me tonight. And I love you for it." I almost thought I detected a tear in Lily's eye as I kissed her. Clyde and John came right over to congratulate us, as did George and Jeremy, Maryanne and David, and all the other guests, really. It was a festive evening to begin with, but Jason certainly cranked it up a notch.

When things had quieted down a bit, I commandeered two glasses of champagne and took Jason aside, as much as it was possible. I said to him, "You're the best birthday gift ever. Jason, please stay with me. I'd die without you."

"Hush, Paul," he said. "I'm not going anywhere, except to take you home."

"What are the social rules concerning the guest of honor pulling a disappearing act?" I asked.

"I think it's frowned upon. But I think Lily and all our friends will forgive us. Can we go home?"

"Yes, please," I said. And that's what we did.

The End

This is a first edition from
Audacity Books
Please visit us on the web at
www.audacitybooks.com
For information, please send your request to
info@audacitybooks.com.

SUCH A GOOD MAN is Volume 3 of Bruce K Beck's **Tolerance Trilogy.** It follows *IT'S THEIR WAY* and *THIS IS GOD'S COUNTRY.* Look for the **Obsession Trilogy—INK OBSESSED, OPERA OBSESSED,** and **LOVE OBSESSED.** And the **Love Trilogy:** Volume 1, *YOU'RE SURE TO FALL IN LOVE*, is set in Provincetown, MA, in the summer of 1976. *LOVE AND THE EPIDEMIC*, set in New York City in 1986, is Volume 2. Volume 3, *AND LOVE ENDURES*, is set in the early 1990s. For updates, and for occasional gifts and offers, please subscribe at:

www.audacitybooks.com/#subscribe

Many thanks to Walter Maas for his generous wisdom. And to Richard Kutner for his classy edits. Tim Barber of Dissect Designs (www.dissectdesigns.com) signed on as a cover designer for my first novel and then became a friend. You're Sure to Fall in Love, indeed. This journey would not have been possible without the example and the teaching of Joanna Penn at www.thecreativepenn.com. I am delighted, Joanna, to add this volume to your long list of books you have enabled. No doubt you will hit your one million mark any day now!

Bruce K Beck is both a writer and an accomplished chef. His novels—including the **Love Trilogy,** the **Obsession Trilogy**, and the **Tolerance Trilogy**—are available online and wherever books are sold. Before turning to fiction, Beck authored ***PRODUCE: A FRUIT AND VEGETABLE LOVERS' GUIDE***, which was called "gorgeous" by ***The New York Times***, "a dazzler" by ***Bon Appetit***, and "the most spectacular food book of the year" by ***The Boston Globe***. His next book was ***THE OFFICIAL FULTON FISH MARKET COOKBOOK***, which was called "invaluable" by Jacques Pépin, and "a treasure" by Irene Sax of ***Newsday***. And Rex Reed said, ". . . you'll love this book. It's like a movie!"